E M I _ _ _ _ _ T T

MW01109745

SEASON
OF GRAY

outskirtspress
DENVER, COLORADO

Season of Gray
All Rights Reserved.
Copyright © 2013 Emily Garrett
v2.0

Cover Photo © 2013 JupiterImages Corporation. All rights reserved - used with permission.

Outskirts Press, Inc.
http://www.outskirtspress.com

ISBN: 978-1-4787-2154-3

Outskirts Press and the "OP" logo are trademarks belonging to Outskirts Press, Inc.

PRINTED IN THE UNITED STATES OF AMERICA

For His Glory.

"However, I consider my life worth nothing to me; my only aim is to finish the race and complete the task the Lord Jesus has given me- the task of testifying to the Good news of God's grace."Acts 20:24

CHAPTER 1

Black and White. Grayscale. Those two settings were the only ones we used. Lucas said they made life look simpler, happier. I used to laugh at that thought. Now I think he was exactly right; color messed everything up. It made reality seem like it was slapping you in the face and constantly reminding you of the parts of your life you would rather leave behind, because you were terrified that if you faced them, you would see that the ones you loved weren't so perfect after all.

Lucas Masterson. Five months ago, I would smile and a giggle would escape my lips. He was six foot, with light chocolate brown eyes and shaggy brown hair that he combed to the side. He was also the captain of the hockey team, vice president of student council, and on every girl's radar list; but by some miracle, he chose me. But if you say his name now, I will look away, my eyes will fill with water that isn't supposed to be there, and if there is an easy way out, I would be the one to take it. That name sends shivers down my spine and my heart feels like it is being pierced over and over by a knife… because five months ago, I lost him.

I still remember it vividly. The pillar of smoke that touched the already dark sky filled every one of my dreams. I remember watching the news and Jim whatever his last name is, was talking about a one-car wreck. From his reports, it looked like a car had lost control on the frontage road of Highway 121, before flying off the road into a nearby tree.

Lucas's car was now showing on the screen, the front of it crumpled by the impact. The words at the bottom of the screen felt like they were getting bigger and bigger: YOUNG MAN KILLED. I remember thinking, it wasn't possible. He couldn't be gone... Lucas, my Lucas. My personal star was shattered and had dispersed all across the galaxy. When I start thinking about that night, my mind usually wanders to the last conversation, the last touch, the last kiss...

"I really have to go." He said the words, but I could tell he didn't mean them by the way he leaned down to kiss me again. I smiled and put my hands on his chest and pushed him away. I climbed out of his lap and smiled at the expression on his face.

"Stop it. Your mom is going to kill you if you don't get home soon."

I looked over at the clock and saw 9:40. That should give him plenty of time to make it to his big white house before 10. I gasped as he pulled me back down on his lap and cradled me to his chest. This was as close to heaven as I had ever been. I tilted my head back and he responded by kissing my lips a little too roughly. By the way his hands moved towards the bottom of my shirt, I could guess what he was trying to do. My suspicions were confirmed when he pulled my shirt up to my belly button. I unlocked my hands from his hair instantly and sighed. I pushed away from him again. I stood up and looked at him. This time instead of pulling me down, he stood up.

"Why do you always stop me so soon?" He smiled down at me, but a frown was pulling at the corners of his mouth. I just shrugged.

"I'm not ready. Why do you always have to ruin it by trying to force me to be ready?" I was starting to get a little hurt by his actions night after night; it's like that's all he wants from me.

"I know you're ready. Guess we could try tomorrow." He looked down at his watch. I just shook my head at him.

"I'm. Not. Ready. So no, we aren't going to try. If you're only going to come over just for that, you might as well not come." I crossed my arms, but couldn't help but smile when he put his arms around my waist and pulled me to his chest. He leaned down and kissed me gently, before he leaned down to whisper in my ear.

"I love you." I stood frozen; did he just say what I think he said? He smiled at me while I stood speechless. He kissed my forehead and walked over to my balcony just like every other night. He would usually do some ridiculous bow or recite something from Romeo and Juliet before climbing over, but tonight was different. He was at the balcony, but he was no longer smiling; it almost looked like he was deep in thought. He climbed onto the railing of the balcony and glanced at me one last time, then shook his head like he was fighting with himself about something. Then with one lithe move, he was gone. I wanted to call out "I love you, too," but I couldn't find my voice. It had abandoned me. But did I really love him?

I rolled around in my bed and woke up sweating. I didn't realize my eyes were wet until I felt the tears overflow. I wanted him here in my room again. I wanted his arms around me to comfort me when I needed him. But those days were over. It was now August and tomorrow I would start my junior year. I shuddered at the thought of having to see the school we once walked around in together, to see all his old friends and all of mine. I had completely closed off from them over the summer to give me time alone to prepare mentally for what I was going to experience the first day of school. At least, that was my excuse.

But the hardest thing I was going to face was to see a remembrance plaque outside the school that read, "In loving memory of Lucas Masterson. Loving son, faithful friend, loyal team mate…" and then smack dab at the bottom of the plaque, there was his hockey picture from junior year. I was almost 100% successful at not showing any emotion when thinking about him, but I wasn't sure if it would be the same when everyone asked me about him. I had received many emails, calls, letters, and texts all asking the same thing. 'How are you doing?' 'How are you holding up?' 'Did you forget yet?' Or the one I really hated, 'Meet someone else, it will take your mind off him.' I never understood what they wanted me to say, so I just never responded. My head was spinning with so many different thoughts and I didn't even realize it when they turned into dreams.

CHAPTER 2

I woke up to the sound of my alarm blaring. I smacked it down, groaning. I looked out my window and saw the start of a new day in Raymertown, New York. I looked over to the corner of my room where the rocking chair stood, where my own personal heaven used to be. Now it was just a big sign reminding me that my boyfriend died. It wasn't really the perfect way to get you in the mood for the first day of school. I walked downstairs in my sweatpants and tank top. My parents had already left for work, but hadn't forgotten to leave a note.

> *Katie-*
> *Have a good first day. Try to start over,*
> *forget about everything.*
> *We love you.*
> *Mom and Mike*

There was the second slap in the face today. I jumped when the coffee maker beeped telling me the coffee was done. I walked past the newspaper that had been casually opened to the new article about Lucas's accident. For some reason, the officials found it necessary to solve why he crashed. They were testing for drugs and drinking while driving. How insane is that?

He had never touched a drug or even thought about drinking a beer. Why were they wasting their time? I started to think about the question that always filled my head. The question that tormented me every second of every day was would he be here right now, holding my hand, if he had left my house five minutes earlier? He might have felt rushed that night trying to get home. But that thought always had an echo that shouted at me and was impossible to block out. It always screamed, "why didn't you tell him you loved him? It was your last chance."

I felt like I was in a trance when I walked back upstairs to get dressed. When I was in my room, I walked over to my closet that was overflowing with old, worn out clothes. I decided to go with my newest shirt and a 'Carpenter Vineyard' hoodie, my dad's vineyard. As I slipped my jacket on, I made my way over to my jewelry box and opened it. I froze. I forgot I stashed all my pictures of Lucas in there to get them out of the way. My therapist had said to remove all traces of that person, it would help the pain; but I couldn't just throw them away.

I could feel my eyes watering up as I pulled the stack of pictures out. The top one was of us sitting on his dirt bike. He had been racing since he was little, but when he found hockey was the sport he really loved, he put his dirt bike dreams on the back burner. Nevertheless, he had always been determined to teach me how to ride it, and one of the times that stood out was the weekend he raced in the Amateur National Motocross Championships, which he raced in every year.

"Okay, Katie. You ready?" He had a broad smile on his lips.

"Not really. I didn't even agree to this!"

"Oh, come on! You agreed to come out to the race track today. You didn't think I would try to teach you?"

He had already gotten me to sit down on the seat with the big bulky helmet on my head. He was now standing in front of me with the front wheel between his legs as he leaned on the handle bars. I looked down at his bike, which was a green and black 250R-PitBull Scrambler. Lucas was wearing his green, black, and white Fox racing pants that led up to a black v-neck.

"No, I thought you were coming here to race for a spot in the motocross tournament thing."

"First of all, it's the Amateur National Motocross Championships and I already have a spot in it. I've been racing in it since I was eleven. I came here for the practice race, but that's not until later. So for now, can I please just teach you to ride?" I nodded reluctantly.

After two hours of learning to ride, I didn't fall off as much, but actually going around the track was difficult. The only reason we stopped was because some of the riders that were going to be participating in the race started arriving and with the riders arriving, so did the fangirls. Lucas rolled his bike back to his trailer.

We were sitting down at one end of the trailer when three fangirls came running up. They asked for pictures and autographs from Lucas.

"You're like my favorite rider. I go to the Motocross Championships every year just to see you!" said one blonde. She was a little taller than me and wore braces.

Lucas just smiled and said, "Aw, that's sweet. Thank you." He reached over and gave her a hug.

A girl with black hair wearing black rimmed glasses said, "I'm in love with you. I watch all your interviews over and over again after you win races."

Lucas chuckled, "Thanks for the support, it means a lot." Then he reached over and gave her a hug, too.

The third girl was the shortest of them all and had dirty blonde hair. She wore a green v-neck shirt that had the number 11 on the front of it, Lucas' racing number. She just shrugged and said, "We're going to get married one day." Then she walked over to him and gave him a kiss on the cheek. After that, the three girls walked off together. I looked over at Lucas with one eyebrow raised.

He just chuckled and stated, "Katie, they're fans. They're at every one of my races. Trust me."

"I know, I know, but——"

Lucas interrupted me. "But nothing, you're my girlfriend. These girls mean nothing to me. I don't even look at them like that."

"But they're beautiful, they come to all your races, and they know what the rules of motocross are!"

Lucas chuckled, "You know, you being jealous is actually kind of hot." I sighed and started to walk away from him, but he grabbed my hands and pulled me back towards him. "Come on, don't be like that. Yeah, I admit some are pretty and make me laugh."

"Oh, good, I'm glad." I didn't try to hide the sarcasm in my voice.

Lucas gave a frustrated sigh. "Let me finish. You want to know why you amaze me so much? It's because you can sit through an entire small-scale music convention with an open mind about every singer that goes up there. I love the look on your face when you really like a song because your eyebrows raise slightly. But I also love the look on your face when you wish a singer would get off the stage. You scrunch up your nose and just stare up at the stage. You're hilarious. I've never met a girl sweeter than you——"

"Okay, you're forgiven. You can stop talking now." Lucas started laughing as he put one of his arms around my waist and pulled me close into a tight hug. He pressed me up against the trailer and kissed me deeply. When an announcer called his heat, he pulled away and got his green, black, and white striped Fox racing shirt out of the front seat of his truck and slipped it on over his v-neck. He came over and kissed me on the cheek before grabbing his bike and rolling it to the starting line.

I sighed and threw the pictures down, scattering them across the hardwood floor that had been spotless moments before. I put my hair up into a quick ponytail and threw my messenger bag over my shoulder. I practically sprinted out to my car just to get away from the scattered pictures of him. I couldn't think his name, or see his face; at least not moments before I would have to put on a brave face to others.

As I pulled into the school parking lot, I could see people laughing with their friends and joking around. Then when they turned and looked at me, pity filled their eyes. I didn't want pity; that wouldn't help at all. I knew they would think of me as the girl who lost her boyfriend. No, I couldn't let them. I had to fake it, at least until I got home.

As I pulled into the parking space that would belong to me for the rest of the year, I noticed one of the new yellow Hummers. I couldn't help but stare at the car. I thought I would remember a car like that from last year, so it had to be new. I could hear guys walking by it whispering and whistling about the car. They would remember it for sure. That meant one thing. New people. I sighed and hopped out of my car. I didn't have time to fix my expression into a smile before I was bombarded with questions from Mattie, the loudest and most obnoxious of my friends.

"Katie! Katie! Oh my Gosh, I haven't seen you in f-o-r-e-v-e-r." I wanted to roll my eyes at the exaggerated forever. It hadn't been that long, only four months. It wasn't long before Mattie realized I was in my own little world. "Hello! I think I deserve a little hello at least. I was worried about you. How have you been?"

There was my cue. I put on a fake smile as big as I could make it and said, "I've been great. I've been meaning to call you, but I've been so busy..." I sighed in relief when the bell rang, signaling us to go to class. "Well, we can catch up later; I have to go to calculus." I smiled at her, walked through the open doors to my classroom and took a seat up front, determined to not let my mind wander off. When Mr. Garner walked in and started passing out papers, I could feel eyes on my back. I didn't want to turn around to face the entire classroom. Instead, I folded my hands on top of my desk and only looked up when Mr. Garner came by my desk and handed me my worksheet. He stood there long enough for me to look up into his eyes filled with pity. He said, "I'm deeply sorry for your loss."

I cringed slightly, hoping he didn't notice. Not him, too. Did everyone know about what happened? There may as well have been posters up on the wall shouting the news to everyone. I couldn't take it anymore; I was about to crack. I grabbed my things and walked out of the class. I didn't know where I was going to go. I just trudged down the hallway looking down at the floor as I went. As I rounded the corner to go to my locker, I ran into someone. Looking straight ahead, all I could see was his shirt. An ordinary blue button-down shirt with sleeves rolled up to his elbows. I let my eyes go down to the rest of his outfit of tan cargo shorts and white vans on his feet. As I brought my gaze up to his face, I saw a slim silver chain around his neck with a cross hanging from it. That brought a tiny smile to my face, a real one; I didn't have to fake it. But the smile vanished in a minute. He cleared his throat and I looked up at his face. I was about to say something when I lost my voice. I stared into the bluest eyes I had ever seen. They were bluer than the ocean. His black hair was medium length and just long enough for him to comb it to the side.

I looked down at my books. "Sorry…I wasn't watching where I was going. I didn't mean to…" I stopped talking when I heard the sound of him chuckling. Was he laughing?

I looked up at him as he met my confused expression. He smiled at me, although it wasn't a full smile. Only one corner of his mouth was pulled up. In spite of that, I felt my heart skip a beat.

"Don't worry about it. It was my fault, just as much as it was yours. No harm done." I was sure I still had the same idiotic, confused look on my face. This school year wasn't starting out so great. It seemed that today I've already made myself look like an idiot too many times. I was catching my breath to introduce myself when I heard someone call a name. Now at least I knew what his name was.

"Chase." He looked over my head, which made

me turn around to see who it was. Of course, it was Brittany, the queen bee. She had her hands on her hips and her light blonde hair curled to just above her shoulders. He looked down at me and smiled. Then walked past me to the waiting wannabe. I shook my head in disbelief. Of course he would already know her. He had to be new to the school. I had known everyone last year, at least by their faces, and I was pretty sure I wouldn't have forgotten that one. I stared after them. As the bell rang, I stood by myself in the now noisy hallway, so I started to head to my next class. I couldn't remember the last time I walked to class by myself. I always had Lucas there with me.

"Can you believe we're already juniors?" Lucas asked as we walked hand in hand into the school.

I looked up at him as I responded, "No. The past few years have been going by so fast!"

Lucas squeezed my hand and leaned down to whisper in my ear, "You ready?" I nodded as he started to lead me down the band hallway that was always empty on the first day of school. Every morning last year, we would go to the place we first met and Lucas would kiss me. To my friends it sounded really dorky, but to us, it was a tradition. As we walked across the school, we didn't get as many stares from students anymore. We were the couple to watch all last year and everyone had been waiting for something to go wrong. After all, I focused on my school work while Lucas was the jock; people didn't think we were very compatible. At first we didn't think we had a lot in common either, other than the fact that instead of listening to the major bands, we preferred to go to small music tours to listen to singer-songwriters who cared more about what kind of music they were making than how much money they could make off it. I enjoyed music like Alexz Johnson and Thomas Fiss, whereas he liked music by Alex Goot and Vampire Weekend, but we both really enjoyed Boyce Avenue. We finally made it to our spot. It was the corner between the choir room and the band room. Lucas leaned down and kissed me lightly before the bell rang. Then we quickly went our separate ways.

CHAPTER 3

When I walked into the front door of my house, the smell of my mom's cooking wafted over me. I had planned to sneak up to my room to get some alone time when I got inside, but my mom had a different idea. I sighed as she called my name.

"Katie, will you come in here, please?" I walked in slowly with a smile plastered on my face.

"How was your first day at school?" She was smiling and looked like she was buying my attempt at a smile.

"Great, Mom, it felt good to see everyone again." I smiled and gave her a little shrug. Shrugging was good; it was easy to fake. She looked like she was buying that, too. I was praying that she wouldn't bring Lucas up again because I knew I wouldn't be able to fake it. I had been doing that all day at school and I couldn't fake it anymore.

She smiled, "I'm glad you were able to act like yourself again. I told you that you could be happy without Lucas." There it was. Just hearing his name makes the wound in my heart pound and punctures my whole left torso. The pain was almost enough to make me want to lie down on the floor and beg to die, but I had to be strong. I couldn't give away my well played charade. Lucas...I forced myself to think his name, even though it made the wound hurt more.

"Mom, please. Not now." I looked at her hoping the strength was still in my eyes. She just frowned.

"Katherine. The sooner you start talking about it and move away from the past, you will see that moving on will be easier and less self-sacrificing." I just shook my head.

"You don't know what you're talking about. I'm doing just fine. I—"

I stopped when my mom cut me off.

"Fine? Moping around isn't fine. You may be fooling your friends at school, but you're not fooling me. He's on your mind all the time. Get him out of your head! Honey, I love you. That's why I'm being so hard on you. You need to move on. Goodness, I can't believe I'm saying this…" She took a deep breath and looked at me, tears filling her eyes. "Lucas is dead, Katie. He's not coming back. It's time for you to make your own path. Make some new friends, start over."

With tears pouring out of my eyes, I leaned my head against the wall and surrendered. I had been trying to be strong way too long. I let all the hurt and pain wash through me and cried it out. I barely noticed my mom putting her arms around me and I buried my face into her shoulder. I didn't notice my stepdad, Mike, come into the kitchen and turn off the stove. I don't know how long I stood there crying, but soon the tears started to dry up. My eyes were red and my head was aching.

My mom looked at me, her own eyes red. "Your Father would be more than happy to let you move there for a little while, if it helps." I couldn't say anything. I started to back out of the room. When I started walking up the stairs, Mike followed me to the bottom of the stairs.

"Kat, remember. The only thing worse than feeling like you can't move on, is the moment you realize you can." I smiled as I remembered that line from one of the shows we used to watch together. I went to my room and fell on my bed. I didn't realize how exhausted I really was until I started to fall asleep.

When I woke up, I looked at my clock. It was 11:30 the next morning. I was about to rush out of the house and go to school when I realized it was Saturday. I never understood why they insisted on making the first day of school on a Friday. I sighed and sat on the edge of my bed. I grabbed a pair of sweats and a T-shirt and went into the bathroom. After my hair was brushed, my teeth were clean and I was dressed, I walked into my room to clean up all the pictures of Lucas and me that were spread out across my floor. I put them all in a stack and walked over to my closet. I glanced down at the picture that was on top and saw a picture of Lucas and me on a plane. We were on our way to visit his grandmother during Christmas break our sophomore year.

"Did you see that?" Lucas was reaching across me to point out of the plane window at the growing storm that was now below us. I looked out to try to see what he was pointing at, but he leaned back and said, "You missed it."

"What was I supposed to be looking for?" I asked as I turned to face him.

"It was lightning. Since we're flying above the storm, you could see lightning going down towards the ground. It was really cool." I turned back towards the window and watched the storm unravel below us.

When the plane landed, I started to get nervous. One of the most important people in Lucas' life was his grandmother and I was now finally getting the opportunity to meet her.

As we were walking to get our luggage, Lucas cleared his throat before looking down at me.

"By the way, you're going to be the first girl that I bring to meet my grandma, so she is very excited to meet you."

"Geez, thanks. Like I wasn't already nervous enough to meet her!"

I shook my head to get the memory out. I quickly set the pictures down at my feet and decided that I needed to get out of the house. I let out a sigh of relief as I climbed into my red Camaro and drove to the diner across the street from my neighborhood. I took a corner booth and started to look at the menu when someone climbed into the seat across from me. That someone was wearing a purple Hurley shirt and a familiar gold chain with a cross hanging from it.

When I looked up, I saw Chase. I was temporarily confused. I started to think of all the reasons why he would want to sit with me, but instead of waiting for him to talk first, I blurted out "Hey!" I wanted to smack myself in the head. I could have come up with several ways to greet him, but I chose the one that sounded the stupidest. I was relieved when I heard his already familiar chuckle.

"Hello. Remember me? The jerk that ran into you yesterday, then left before he introduced himself." He smirked at me, like he did yesterday. For some reason, I couldn't help but smile.

I giggled a little. "How could I forget you? You're the first jerk I've met in a while."

His eyes widened, "I...I didn't mean to... I had things to take care of. I'm—" He stopped talking when I started laughing.

"I'm kidding. I'm Katie, by the way." He breathed a sigh of relief and smiled.

"Chase. It's nice to meet you, Katie."

He looked around and saw Brittany waving at him from her fancy convertible. He sighed, then looked at me and smiled. "Well, I better get going. See you around."

"I didn't picture you as the type of guy that rode in a convertible."

He chuckled. "I'm usually not. I drive a yellow hummer."

"I can see you in something like that. Well you better get going. See you later." I waved a little, then put my hand down and sighed. He was a very handsome guy, but if he chose the kind of girls that put everyone else down to make themselves look good, then I didn't want to have anything to do with him.

CHAPTER 4

On Monday, I woke up late and almost got to school late. I walked into my calculus class and saw everyone watching me very carefully, like I was going to run out again. I sat down in my seat and scrunched down as far as I could. Mr. Garner walked in the classroom and told us that he would be giving us a lecture. While the rest of the class groaned, I was thrilled. A lecture meant a boring hour, but it also meant no questions, which would be a nice break.

When the bell rang, I walked out of the classroom and down the hall. I saw Chase walking toward me so I turned the other way. I didn't want to be seen talking with him with so many of Brittany's spies everywhere. Staying away from him didn't last very long though.

I thought I had been doing a fairly good job of avoiding him, but at the end of the day when I was walking out of my last class, someone came up and walked beside me. When I looked up to see who it was, I saw Chase's blue eyes staring down at me with the beautiful smile that made my knees weak every time I saw it. I couldn't say anything and was happy when he opened his mouth to speak.

"If I didn't know any better, I would say you have been avoiding me." As he said those words, the smile reached his eyes. All I could do was shrug. I didn't trust my voice, much less what my brain was about to make me say.

He took that as a confirmation and he just nodded. "I guess I was a jerk the first time, so I deserve it." He looked ahead of him when he said that, and slid his hands into his jacket pockets. I reached out and touched his shoulder. When I touched him, he stopped walking and turned towards me; almost like my touch made him freeze. I glanced at my hand quickly and stopped walking.

I said, "It's not that I didn't want to talk to you, but you keep ditching me and I just didn't want your girlfriend getting upset." Just as quickly as it had come, his smile faded and confusion filled his eyes.

"Girlfriend? Am I missing something?" He looked around then back down at me.

"Isn't Brittany your–?" I couldn't finish my sentence because he started laughing, and I glanced up at him. He was a couple inches taller than me, so I had to tilt my head up to look at him.

"Brittany is my cousin. Since I'm new in town, her mom is making her show me around. Plus, even if she wasn't my cousin, she isn't my type." He smiled at me and I felt a sudden joy inside. Why was I so happy? Did I even know this guy? I shrugged it off.

"Oh, well. Now I feel dumb." I could feel my cheeks getting red while Chase started to look uncomfortable.

"Look, I know you may not want to talk about it, but I've been hearing some things about you." Oh, man. He knew. I wasn't ready for him to see the water works. "And…your boyfriend." All I could do was look at him, and then I began walking toward my car. He took that as confirmation that I wanted him to follow me. When I got to my car, I turned around.

"What do you want to know about it?" I asked. I was fine with talking about it outside, where I had my car to take cover in if I needed to. Chase looked down at the ground and rested his hand on the hood of my car.

"Well, I was wondering if you were over it; if you had moved on." He slid his hands into his pockets, which I figured was what he did when he felt uncomfortable. I thought about my answer very carefully; I didn't want to say anything wrong.

I sighed and responded, "I don't know, Chase. I can't forget something like that and just throw it over my shoulder." He nodded and gently wiped a tear from my cheek that had escaped my well-guarded eyes.

"I wasn't expecting you to forget about it. I don't know, Katie. I feel…different around you. Better than I have in a long time. I don't know what it is about you." I was shocked. I had not been expecting that. But unlike four months ago, my voice wasn't lost; and unlike four months ago, I wasn't going to lose my chance at saying what needed to be said.

"You were honest with me; you deserve for me to be honest." I took a deep breath to steady myself. "I feel better around you. When you're not around, it feels like the burden is a thousand times heavier. When you're around, I still feel the burden, but it feels lighter. So you asked if I'm over it. I don't think I'm close to being over it, so if you aren't ready for a broken person that might need fixing, you shouldn't waste your time."

I looked down at the ground not wanting him to walk away; but at the same time, I didn't want him to stay and waste his time with someone who couldn't give him one hundred percent. I felt a warm gentle hand under my chin forcing me to look at him. What I saw were warm blue eyes and the smile I already loved.

"Everyone needs a little fixing." I smiled as he leaned down and kissed my forehead. As he helped me into my car, I knew what I was feeling. I was so happy I could explode. I was back.

CHAPTER 5

Who is that? I leaned closer towards the rear view mirror checking left and right for any signs that I had changed. No, it was me. But I was smiling. I was happy. I was thrilled that I was back, but something was tugging at my heartstrings. I felt like I was turning my back on Lucas. Isn't this what he would have wanted? For me to be happy, even if it wasn't with him? I tried to remember what I had acted like when I was around Lucas, to bring the real me back, and show Chase everything about me. But I was coming up empty.

And as I stared at the person in the mirror, I was confused. It was me in the mirror, but who was I really? I knew that I needed to find out in order to really be able to move on.

For the next couple of weeks, Chase and I were always together. People started to talk about us dating and girls started to give me dirty looks. It was true. I was happy, but we weren't dating. The burden was still there. I still thought about Lucas all the time, but now I had someone there to help me through it. The more I hung out with Chase, the more I felt like I was betraying Lucas. I usually shook it off when I was with Chase, but it was hard to be in control of my feelings when I was by myself at night.

When I woke up at nine o'clock Saturday morning,

the sun was already streaming into my window. I went
to my closet, which now wasn't as shabby. When Chase
first saw my closet, he thought the clothes looked a
little worn. He had insisted on taking me to the
mall, which I didn't deny because honestly, I knew I
needed it and it was another day with my best friend.
Now I picked out a pair of my favorite jeans and my
school shirt, Carland High. I trudged downstairs after
I brushed my teeth and combed my hair until it was
decent.

My Mom and my stepdad, Mike, were sitting side
by side on the couch. I was used to the idea that my
mom and dad's marriage hadn't worked out and I was
happy that she found someone new. Mike was a great
guy. He was tall, about six feet six inches, with light
blonde hair. He was in his mid 40's and always wearing
a hat. He was a nice guy. He just wasn't my father, but
sometimes he acted like it.

I had been acting a lot better and wasn't moping
anymore. I could tell that they were happy for me and
they both seemed to love Chase, because they usually
brought him up in every conversation. I loved talking
about Chase, but sometimes they drew conclusions;
conclusions that weren't supposed to be drawn. I
wasn't dating him. I didn't like him like that. He was
more like my brother. I usually caught myself thinking
of him like a guardian angel, there to help me back on
my feet.

When I got to the bottom of the stairs, both adults

on the couch turned toward me. Mike smiled his usual smile. "Morning, Kat." And to my mom, "Look who's up." My mother laughed a little and shook her head. "Why are you up so early, honey? Surely you don't have a date this early."

I was walking toward the kitchen, but froze when she said that. "Date? Mom, you go on dates with your boyfriend, which I don't have."

"Katie, Chase can't be just a friend. I see the way you look at him." She smiled lightly at me.

I just shook my head angrily. "He isn't my boyfriend! He is my best friend! In case you haven't noticed, I feel better because of him. Because of his friendship! I'm not expecting anything more from him because I don't want anything more."

I turned around and started walking toward the front door. I looked at my watch and saw that it was 9:30. "I'm going to Chase's...you know, my friend." I didn't hear her reply because I slammed the door before she had time to object. It was pouring outside, so I quickly ran to my car. As I slid into the front seat, I turned the key in the ignition, but before I drove off, I looked up at the gray sky and murmured, "Great." I hated driving in the rain. It was hard to see and I just didn't like it. I sat in the driveway for a few minutes waiting for the rain to die down. As I sat there, I started thinking about the first time my parents met Lucas. It was a few weeks after we went to a music tour in our freshman year. He was officially my boyfriend then, so

Mike thought it would be best if I invite him over for dinner.

"So, Lucas, tell us about yourself." We had all just sat down for dinner. Mike had grilled pork chops, my mom had made garlic mashed potatoes, and I had made the salad all before Lucas showed up. So by the time he came through the door, we were all ready for dinner; which I wasn't complaining about because then you don't have the awkward questions that always come before dinner.

Lucas cleared his throat, "I'm currently Vice President of the freshman class, captain of my hockey team, and I'm on the honor roll."

Mike just looked at him. "Okay, that's good to know, but tell us about you. Not about everything you've earned or what your standing is in school. That doesn't tell us who you are. We don't judge, don't worry." Mike gave him a cheesy grin.

Lucas chuckled. "I understand. Well, I love music. I play guitar. I'm not afraid to admit I like some chick flicks." Mike and my mom started laughing, but Lucas kept talking. "I've always wanted to go to Africa. I used to do a lot of motocross before hockey. Now I only do races a few times a year, but I love getting out on the track anytime I can. That's all I have for now." Lucas had a huge smile on his face. I looked over at Mike, who by that time had set his fork down.

"Since you know about dirt bikes, do you know a lot about motorcycles?"

"Yeah, I want to get one, but my mom freaks about the idea."

"Well, I have my old 1976 Yamaha 100cc motorcycle from when I was in high school out in the garage. It doesn't run. The engine is busted and I can't figure out what's wrong with it. If you want, I could really use a second pair of eyes to check it out." I could see Mike glowing. The motorcycle was his baby. He loved that thing. I knew Lucas was on his good list because now Mike had someone to talk with about motorcycles.

"No way? That's so cool. Those are first editions. What color?"

"It's a bright red. Well, it was. It's more of a rustic red now."

Lucas replied, "Well, I'll definitely help you. Just let me know when." I looked over at my mom, who was staring at me with a smile set on her lips. I smiled back before looking back down at my food.

"Why don't we go check it out now?" Mike quickly stood up and went out into the garage.

Lucas gave me a quick glance before looking over at my mom and said, "Excuse me."

When Lucas stood up, my mom said, "Of course. Do you want an extra pair of clothes, just in case he puts you to work?" Lucas smiled and looked down at his black Nikes, his faded blue jeans and red button-down shirt with rolled up sleeves, and thin white tie.

"No, ma'am, my clothes will do just fine. Thank you, though." Lucas looked at me again before walking into the garage. As soon as Lucas closed the door, I picked up my plate and took it to the sink. As I turned back to face my mom, she was staring at me with a smile on her lips.

"Why are you looking at me like that?" I folded my arms across my chest.

My mom just shrugged, "Oh, nothing." She got up from the table and stacked the dirty plates on top of each other, then turned to me. "I like him. He seems to have a good head on his shoulders, and he handled himself very well when Mike decided to interrogate him."

I smiled, "I hope it impressed Mike."

"Well, it impressed me." My mom smiled as she picked the plates up off the table before taking them to the kitchen.

I didn't want to think about him right now; I couldn't. So I put my car in drive and drove to the only place I wanted to be. A couple minutes later, I got to Chase's house. His mom's car was gone. I figured she had to work at the Children's Hospital today and since his dad had ditched him and his mom a few years before, I knew Chase was home by himself. I stopped my car and got out.

I loved what his mom had done to the front of his

house. It was beautiful. She had big green bushes lining the front with many different colored flowers mixed in them. His mom was a nurse at the hospital, but Chase had told me her dream was to open her own business as a landscape artist. He had always said he was going to buy her a store when he got enough money.

I walked up and rang the doorbell. When nobody answered, I rang it again. I was starting to wonder if Chase was even home. It was hard to tell since I couldn't see his yellow H3 Hummer, which he always parked in the garage.

I saw some movement on the stairs through the window at the side of the door and smiled at him when he opened the door. He was in a pair of sweatpants with no shirt. His usually perfect shaggy hair was going in all directions.

I laughed. "I'm guessing I woke you up." When he gave me his usual half smile, I sighed. It was the smile I was growing to love.

"Just a little. Come in." When I walked in, he engulfed me in a bear hug and I giggled.

"Chase! It's too early." I laughed and pushed against his chest. He led the way to his bedroom, which was upstairs by his huge game room and the farthest room down the hall. In his game room, he had a pool table and a poker table. Then when you walked into his bedroom, there was a big 42-inch plasma TV which was fully equipped with Xbox 360 that he rarely played when I was over. He went over to his closet and pulled out a black crew cut shirt and put it on before laying down on his bed. I sat down on his futon. His room was always so spotless; everything was where it was supposed to be. I never knew how he got all this stuff…all this expensive stuff. It must have cost him a fortune. I didn't realize I had been looking out of the window blankly for a couple of minutes until he cleared his throat.

"So is there a reason you came over? Or do you just enjoy waking me up early on a Saturday?" He smiled at me. I reached over and grabbed a pillow that was on his futon and threw it at him, which he easily caught.

"I can leave if sleeping is more important than me," I teased as I stood up and started walking toward the door. But then a hand was on my wrist pulling me back.

"No, I was kidding. You can stay. You know you're welcome here." That made me smile. I was happy I had a place to go if I ever needed to escape. I had been spending so much time here that I felt just as safe here as I did in my own house. I smiled over at Chase. As usual, Chase chuckled and responded, "What?"

I shrugged as I said, "I was just remembering the conversation I had with Amelia yesterday. The one I told you about in the car…" I could tell he didn't remember what I was talking about by the way he just sat there staring out the window. I laughed and said, "About her calling you a flirt."

"I remember. I'm so not a flirt. She's crazy." I stared at him in disbelief.

"You're joking, right? You are such a flirt. Every girl you see you do that…" I pointed to his face and did a flowing motion around his eyes…"thing with your eyes. That sucks them in." He gave me his half smile and I laughed. Suddenly, he stopped laughing and went serious.

"No, but come on! That's not flirting! That's…" He paused to think of a word that would end up being completely wrong and would somehow make him look like the victim. I was happy when he shrugged and a huge smile pulled up the corners of his lips. "Yeah, I got nothing. But who cares. It's flirting. Shoot me, I'm a guy." I just rolled my eyes.

"I'm a girl. You don't see me walking through the halls sticking my chest out." We both laughed a little and sat in his room and talked about whatever came into our minds. I still haven't told him the full story about Lucas. He only knows that he died and how. He doesn't know the details or how long it took me to get over Lucas. He doesn't even know about all the dreams I constantly have of Lucas. I didn't really feel the need to tell him because most guys, best friend or not, just want the overview. They don't want the details, so even if I took the time to explain all the boring details, he wouldn't remember them. I started to look around the room and my eyes stopped at his calendar. I had forgotten that I was almost done with my junior year and it was almost spring break.

"Do you have any plans for spring break?" I looked

towards Chase waiting for his response. He shrugged.

"No, not really… What about you?" I was going to say no, but my phone started ringing. I hesitantly picked it up when the caller ID said 'Daddy.' I pressed the 'connect call' button.

"Hey, Dad."

"Katie! Hey, baby. What are you doing for spring break? I just moved into my new house. I bought that ranch we always talked about having. What do you say about coming up and spending the week with me? It's been awhile." I could almost see his smile and I couldn't say no to my dad. The last time I had seen him was Christmas. Almost three months.

I looked towards Chase before answering, then said, "Sure, Dad…that sounds like fun. I'll be up first thing after school Friday. Text me the address, will you? Bye, Dad. I love you." Then I disconnected the call.

I looked at Chase as he said, "Well, that answers my question."

CHAPTER 6

Friday came too fast. The week flew by and I felt like everything was blurring past me and not slowing down enough for me to see anything or to experience anything. When the bell rang letting us out of school for spring break, I walked out to my car which already had all of the bags I would need for the week long stay at my Dad's.

I was about to climb into my car when I saw Chase jogging over. He stopped a couple times to hug the girls saying goodbye to him. I rolled my eyes and stopped counting the girls after five. When he finally got to me, he gave me his usual smile. It was *my* smile. I never saw him use it on anyone else but me.

"I still can't believe you're leaving me for a whole week." He shook his head as he looked down at me.

"Hey, don't let me ruin your spring break. I'm sure you have a lot of girls that would love to hang out with you. Ask one of them." I smiled at him when he started chuckling.

"Tempting, but they aren't you." He reached down to hug me and I wrapped my arms around his neck. I knew I was going to miss him and would probably catch myself thinking about him. I started to pull away after a couple of seconds, but he held me there. Finally, he pulled back, but kept holding on to my waist. He looked down into my eyes and started to lean his head down. I knew what he was trying to do, so I shyly turned my head and pushed against his chest.

"Chase. Please." I looked up at my best friend and could clearly see the rejection on his face. He stared at me, so I said, "I'm not ready." He looked at me in disbelief.

"It's been six months. So either you're taking a long time to get over Lucas or you're so used to acting like you're not ready that you don't even see that you are." I stared at him and took a deep breath. I could have exploded, but I didn't want this to be our last conversation before I drove away.

"I told you the day after we met that I was broken. I warned you. It's going to take some time for me to piece myself back together." He nodded and I could tell he understood.

"I'm sorry, Katie. I didn't mean to rush you. Take your time. I'll be here when you are ready." He smiled and gave me a gentle squeeze one more time.

When he was hugging me, I whispered, "I really wish you wouldn't waste your time." He chuckled as he leaned down and brushed his lips across my forehead before backing away.

"See you Saturday." Then he gave me *my* smile. My perfect, beautiful smile and walked away. That was the memory I wanted to have of him for the next week. That's the memory I would fall back on when I needed it.

And as I drove down the long hilly twisting road leading to my Dad's ranch, I was thankful that my mom thought it necessary to have a GPS system installed in my car. I would have been totally lost without it.

I stopped the car when the road ended at a big gate that said 'Carpenter' which was my dad's last name and mine, too. I refused to change my last name to Mike's, which was 'Hougseten.' There was no way I was going to be Katie Hougseten. Katie Carpenter worked better for me. I opened the car door and instantly knew I was in the country. The outdoor smell came rushing into my car. As I looked at the ground, I saw a trail of yellow dust. My mind wandered back to the first camping trip I went on with my dad.

"Daddy, look. It's fairy dust." I reached down and grabbed a handful of pollen and threw it at him. When he started coughing, I laughed. "You can fly now." He just looked down at me with his wise eyes and laughed.

"You know, Katie, that stuff comes from the flowers." I remember looking down at the dust and not understanding what he meant. Was he trying to say that my fairy dust came from flowers and not Tinkerbelle?

"So the fairies steal it from the flowers? Or do they work together?"

He quickly answered, "They work together." He smiled as he grabbed a handful of the yellow dust that was now changing the color of his shirt from a bright white to a bright yellow and turned to me. "You know, I think the dust will work better on you." He smiled and threw the little bit of pollen he had at my shoes and then he picked me up and spun me around.

The sound of the gate opening interrupted my memory. I was so lost in the past that I had almost forgotten where I was. This ranch used to leave my dad and me speechless. I remember riding horses up here to just look at the entrance of the house we dreamed of one day owning.

I smiled as I finally passed the gates that led down the winding road toward my dad's new estate. I pulled into the driveway and as I parked my car, I saw the big wooden front door swing open and my dad come running out.

"Katie! I can't believe you came!" I had barely made it out of my car before I was engulfed into one of my dad's bear hugs.

"Dad…can't breathe." He dropped me just as the world started spinning. I smiled as he turned me around to look at the huge country house that now belonged to him, and eventually me. The house's big wooden structure was enough to make me gasp, but I think what really did it was the landscaping. I loved how he had bushes that lined the edges of the house, with the thick woods right off the corner. He had a brown porch swing on the long, white porch. But what left me speechless were the huge old fashioned double wood doors that opened up into a large living room with leather couches and chairs. In the center of the living room was a 56-inch plasma screen TV. Off the living area, was an office, out of which I would bet my dad ran his business.

I looked out into the backyard, seeing some of the acres that now belonged to us. All the way to the right was my dad's vineyard. He had always wanted to run a vineyard and now he was able to. I smiled as I realized that even though my dad's marriage with my mom didn't work out, he was still trying to make his dreams reality. My dad wasn't that big of a man. He was just under six feet and weighed about 185 pounds, but most of it was muscle. When he was in high school, he had been the star quarterback and the local track star. He had brown hair with green eyes and wore a lot of khakis with button-down shirts that he tucked in and he always rolled the sleeves up to his elbows. Even when he was out working in the vineyard, he wore the same attire.

That evening my dad and I sat on the porch swing to watch the sunset. I had forgotten how much I missed sitting down in the country with a glass of iced tea watching the sun set over the horizon. How the sun hit the trees makes you want to hit the pause button and sit in paradise. I looked over at my dad and saw the twinkle in his eyes and suddenly missed having him around every day. Knowing that no matter what I went through, if I bombed a test or got in a huge argument with my mom, he would be right there. My dad had always been my escape.

"So, Kat. Any boys got your eye?" He laughed as I looked down at my hands.

"Dad, do you really want to hear all of my boy stories?" I looked up at him as he chuckled and answered me.

"I need to know who I have to beat up." One thing I loved about my dad, he always knew when to drop a subject. When the sun was completely down and my glass of iced tea empty, I started hearing noises from the woods. That was my cue to turn in. I leaned over and kissed my dad on the forehead and went inside. After a quick shower and with my teeth brushed, I went into my room. Everything was exactly how it used to be in his old house. My bed was in the corner by the nightstand. A picture of my dad and me sat proudly on it. I climbed into bed and sank into a deep sleep.

The next morning after we had breakfast in town, my dad had to get back to work on the vineyard, so I decided to tour the small town by myself. I went to the local farmers market for a couple of hours. When my wallet was feeling light and my hands were full of stuff that I thought I had to have though didn't have a reason for why I needed all of it, I walked towards one of the local diners. As I reached to open the door, I didn't realize the door was opening from the inside until it hit me in the head and all of my bags went flying everywhere. I landed on the ground with a *thud* and everything went black.

I woke up a couple of hours later on a comfortable couch in a warm house. I started to move around when a deep voice out of nowhere said, "I'm not sure if you want to move around. You hit your head pretty hard."

I looked frantically around for whoever was talking and saw movement near me. A man walked up and dropped down on his knees beside the couch. He started dabbing my forehead with a cool cloth. From where I was lying, all I could see was his shaggy brown hair, and his breathtaking green and amber eyes.

"What happened?" I choked the words out and then smiled in response to one of the most dazzling smiles I had ever seen. He had shiny white teeth and all of them were super straight. It was a smile that a movie star would kill for.

When he stood up to get the towel wet again, I saw that he was wearing a checkered red and white button-down shirt opened to reveal a white undershirt. He was exceptionally tan and had a leather bracelet around his right wrist and on his other wrist, he was wearing a brown leather watch. He also had on faded blue jeans and white vans that reminded me of Chase's, except this guy's weren't as white. I looked up at his face and saw that he was still smiling.

As he turned back around, he said "Someone hit you in the head with a door. The manager told me to take you back to her place. So here we are." He grinned and said, "I'm sorry, I'm being rude. I'm Bryan and you're Katie, right? I nodded. How did he know who I was? Like he could read my mind, Bryan answered, "I'm not stalking you, I promise. I looked in your wallet to see who to contact. You know, just in case. I know your dad. The whole town knows your dad. He's kind of like a big deal around these parts."

"Are you from around here?" I asked stupidly. I knew I sounded a bit rude, so I was relieved when he didn't take offense to the question.

He just chuckled as he answered, "Yes. I know I'm supposed to wear a cowboy hat and some boots since I live in the country, but most folks here don't dress like that 24/7." He looked at his watch and said, "Well, I should get you home. I wouldn't want your dad to worry." He smiled as he helped me up. He kept his hand on my back in case I lost my balance.

When we got to the front door of the house, he opened the door for me and helped me down the steps. Then when we got to his truck, he opened the passenger door for me and helped me into the passenger side. A guy had never done that for me before. I could really get used to this southern hospitality.

CHAPTER 7

The next morning I woke up to the smell of bacon. I love bacon. As I walked downstairs, the aroma got stronger and when I got to the kitchen, I saw a plate filled with bacon sitting on the island. Without saying anything, I slid a piece off the plate and turned to where it should have been my dad cooking. Instead, a woman stood there. I cleared my throat as she was just beginning to turn around. She jumped a little, then turned completely toward me.

"Oh. I didn't hear you come down. Welcome home, Katie." I just stared at her, not moving. I wasn't sure what to say or do. She didn't look familiar and I didn't think I had an older sister.

I looked her in the eyes and tried to come up with a nicer way to respond, but instead I blurted out, "Who are you?" I smiled after I said it to act like I didn't mean to be rude, but honestly, I didn't care if it sounded rude or not. Why was some strange woman in my dad's house anyway? I looked around the room for my dad to walk in. But after a couple of seconds, I asked "Well?"

She answered me in a stern voice. "Your dad wanted to tell you. I wasn't supposed to say anything. He went out to check on the vineyard and I thought I would surprise him with breakfast, not thinking you would be up yet."

I just nodded, "Okay. Well, I'm going to go to the market."

"Stop!" I cocked my head to the side; did she just yell at me?

I slowly turned around. "Yes?"

"You are going to eat breakfast with your father and me since you're up."

I didn't even know her! She didn't have the right to boss me around.

"Okay... well, maybe instead, I'll go to the market and eat breakfast with strangers. That's basically what this feels like." I was about to turn around and walk out, but the woman spoke before I could.

"You know what? For being such a smart ass, give me your car keys."

"Are you serious? I don't even know you. You know what? Forget it." I walked past her to the back door that led out to the vineyard. After pulling the doors open, I walked outside and ran down the steps. I stopped right on the edge of the vineyard and yelled, "Dad! Where are you?"

I heard him running before he showed up behind the short picket fence and jumped over it.

"What is it? Are you okay?" I noticed how labored his breathing was and I saw how anxious he looked, so I nodded to try to calm him down.

"Who is inside? Is she a maid or something?" I pictured the woman's strawberry blonde hair pulled back into a loose ponytail. I remembered the very short sundress she had on; which could really stand to be one size larger, unless she meant to make her boobs pop out like that.

"Look, I was going to tell you about her last night, but you were so happy. And I didn't know how to tell you."

I suddenly knew what he was implying. "She's your girlfriend?" I looked at him in shock.

"Actually, she's my fiancée. We're getting married in a couple of weeks. I think you will really like her. Her name is Carrie."

I shook my head and ran to my car. I had kept my purse in my car last night. Since we had a gate to get onto the property, I knew it would be safe. I opened my door and slammed it shut as I started the car and drove down the road.

What was he thinking? He couldn't be getting married. Why didn't he tell me? If he lets that woman into our lives, it won't be OUR place anymore because she would be living here, too. It wasn't that I was mad he was getting married. I was just mad at everything she would be destroying. I already dreaded the day when they would walk down the aisle as Mr. and Mrs. Charlie Carpenter.

I stopped the car on the side of the road where I saw a trail that led into the woods. I got out of my car and walked over to investigate and saw that it was a well tended and well worn path. As I made my way up the trail, I started to hear running water. I was trying to figure out where it was coming from, but I couldn't quite place the direction. In the woods, the trees were all so green and huge. They were also close together, making the area almost dark. As I kept walking, the sound of the water kept getting louder until finally I could hear it clearly and saw a little river that ran through the woods. I walked over to it and sat down on a rock.

I don't know how long I sat there until I started hearing something coming from farther down the river that almost sounded like music. At first I thought I was just hearing things, but the sound would stop, and then come back.

As the sound became clearer, I started to recognize it as someone strumming on a musical instrument. I was now very curious, so I climbed down from the rock and started to follow the sound down the river. After a couple of detours due to the river's flow, I saw someone facing away from me and sitting down on a large boulder. I wasn't quite sure who it was because all I could see was the back of him, but I could tell he was wearing a cowboy hat with a black leather jacket. It then occurred to me that the musical instrument was a guitar being expertly strummed and my mind quickly wandered back to the first time I met Lucas.

I walked into school. It was the first day back from Christmas break my freshman year and I was nervous about coming back. I started to make my way to the choir room so I could put my lunch in my locker. As I passed the band hall, I heard someone playing a guitar. As I walked into the hall, I saw it was Lucas Masterson, the freshman homecoming king and the school's varsity hockey team captain. I quickly ducked my head and started to walk out when I heard Lucas ask, "Is someone there?"

I turned around and retraced my steps so he could see me.

"Sorry, I heard something playing and I thought I knew the song. I'll just leave you alone."

"Wait, did you say you knew what song that was?"

I nodded. "If I'm right, it was Beautiful Disaster by Jon McLaughlin. He performed at the singer/songwriter music tour that came into town and played that song. I go every year."

Lucas stood up. "You go to that? You're the first person from this school that I've met who actually knows what it is. I go every year, too."

"No way? That's awesome. Well, I didn't mean to bother you."

"There's one coming up about an hour away from Raymertown. I was going to make it a day trip if you would like to join me."

"Do you even know who I am?"

Lucas chuckled, "You're Katie Carpenter. You sit four seats in front of me in English. You're the smartest one in the class, as far as I know you don't play sports, and you seem to have very good taste in music."

I smiled. "I'm a little predictable, aren't I?"

Lucas raised his eyebrows. "I just pay attention. Well, and going to the same school since second grade helps a little bit." He smiled at me.

"I didn't think you knew who I was…" I trailed off as I blushed lightly.

"Katie, you won the poetry contest two years in a row. If you were trying to go unnoticed, maybe you shouldn't have been so darn good at writing poetry." Lucas gave me a tiny smile.

I nodded. "Well, I better get going. Let me know when the concert is. I'll think about it."

With my mind returning back to the here and now, I took another step toward where the music was coming from, but as I did, I stepped on a branch. Just my luck. The person playing the guitar quickly stopped playing and spun around. As I looked at the person's face, a small smile came to my lips.

"Bryan? What are you doing out here?" My smile widened when he started laughing.

"You know, I could ask you the same question." I took in the black cowboy hat and the shaggy brown hair that was just long enough to stick out behind his ears and curl right above his amber green eyes. His smile looked like the sun could bounce right off it.

"I was just taking a walk."

He set his guitar down against the rock and started walking toward me. As he was doing that he said, "And naturally you would be walking in the middle of the woods."

All I could do was nod as he stopped right in front of me. I hadn't noticed before that Bryan's cologne is very unique. It's almost like Hollister meets Calvin Klein. "At least I have a valid excuse." I just stood there waiting for his answer. While I was waiting for him to respond, I noticed that under his black leather jacket he was wearing a purple and white Zoo York shirt with painter blue jeans and white cowboy boots. Finally, I broke the silence.

"You actually look like you're from around here now." I smiled as I pointed up to his cowboy hat. As I did, he tipped his hat forward like a "howdy, ma'am."

He smiled and said, "Oh, right. Well, I try my best to fit into this little ole' town."

I could tell he was joking because his voice was filled with sarcasm. "Oh, so are you a comedian now? Do you not care about fitting in?"

They were standing near a patch of daisies, so Bryan reached down and picked one up. For a couple of seconds, he didn't look at me. He just stared down at the flower. Then all of a sudden, he spoke.

"This flower. While it comes from a patch of many yellow daisies, each one is unique. Something about it is different from the rest. Same goes for us. Why try to fit in?" He then slowly placed the flower behind my ear and smiled.

I looked up into his eyes and returned his smile. "I've decided I like the cowboy look on you. It works." I chuckled.

He smiled wider as he looked down at me. "Thank you. Wait, are you flirting with me?" He acted shocked as I shook my head, but before I could deny it he said, "My wife would be appalled." I stood there frozen after he said that. How old was he? He couldn't be any older than me.

"You're married?" I asked, still shocked by what he had just said. He suddenly interrupted my train of thought.

"I was kidding, Katie." He laughed lightly. "Do you believe everything people say?"

I shook my head and then remembered the tune he was playing on his guitar.

"What were you playing just now?" I pointed over to his guitar leaning against the rock. He turned to see where I was pointing. "Oh, that. The song is not really finished yet. Actually, not even close." He shrugged loosely and I smiled.

"Will you play it for me?" I asked as I gently took his hand.

"I guess. But it's really not good." He turned and started walking over to his guitar with my hand still in his. Releasing my hand, he picked up his guitar and sat down on the rock. He started strumming the guitar softly. The instrumental part itself sounded amazing, but then he began to sing.

"I don't know where I'd be,

Without you by my side.

I don't think I could make it,

Without you along for the ride."

He finished singing and kept lightly strumming his guitar until finally he stopped. His voice was better than most of the musicians out there today. He sang with force and energy. But it didn't seem like he was singing it to anyone. I couldn't tell if there was passion in it or not.

"I told you there wasn't much to it." He set his guitar down and just looked at me.

"Bryan, that was amazing. Who was it for?" He just shook his head and looked down at his hands.

"I don't know. Nobody right now. That's why I haven't been able to write anymore of it. I don't know what to say, because I don't have any inspiration."

"I'm sure when you find someone to write about, it will be even more amazing."

He smiled and stood up. "Come with me." He grabbed my hand again. "There is something I want to show you. I haven't shown anyone before." He jumped over the stream and then helped me over. As he led me through the woods, I started to get a feeling in the pit of my stomach that we were lost. I could have sworn we passed one of the trees numerous times.

"Where are you taking me?" I looked over at him and he just shook his head.

"You'll see. We're almost there." I started to hear the water again, so I just assumed it was the river, but it was louder than before. Suddenly, we broke through the last of the trees. Instantly the sound of the water was close. I stopped in my tracks when I saw a waterfall. It wasn't huge, but it was perfect anyway. Around it there were flowers; it was a mini meadow. I smiled and looked over at Bryan, who was looking at me. I guessed that he was measuring my reaction.

"It's beautiful." I looked at it again and noticed that we were on a hill. We had to walk down the hill to get to the edge of the waterfall. I took a step forward and didn't see that the hill was muddy because of a recent downpour. I slipped in the mud and slid down the hill on my butt, getting my jeans all muddy. I heard laughter coming from Bryan and looked up at him. I smiled playfully as I grabbed a handful of mud and threw it at him. It landed on the leg of his jeans. He stopped laughing and looked down at me as I started laughing. A mischievous look came over his face as he took off his leather jacket and slipped off his boots and cowboy hat. As I started climbing up the muddy hill, I realized my whole outfit was probably ruined. When I got to the top of the hill, I grabbed his hand and pulled him down the hill with me. When we were all the way to the bottom, his once purple and white shirt was now purple and brown. He stood up and pulled me up with him.

"I'm sorry. I just ruined your shirt." He looked down at his shirt and smiled.

"Don't be, after all, it's just a shirt." He leaned over and picked up a handful of mud and plopped it on my head. When it started dripping down over my face, he chuckled and rubbed it in, being careful to avoid my eyes. I smiled as I leaned down and got a big handful of mud and set it down in a pile on top of his head and then rubbed it into his hair.

"There you go." I laughed.

Suddenly he picked me up and ran back up the hill. When we were at the top, he set me down and then said, "Last one down buys dinner." I laughed as I dove headfirst down the hill. When I got to the bottom, I looked around for him. When I couldn't find him, I looked back up at the top of the hill and saw him smiling at me. Suddenly he dove headfirst down the hill, too. When he got to the bottom, he stood up and walked over to me. "I guess I'm buying." He leaned down and kissed my cheek. He laughed and wiped the mud off that his lips left on my cheek.

"Let's get you washed off." He led me under the waterfall. It was like a shower. He stood by me and started to run his hands through my hair to help the water wash out all the mud. When he was done, I ran my hands through his hair. After I was done, he grabbed the bottom of his shirt and slid it off. I don't know why I never noticed earlier, but Bryan was ripped. He had well defined abs and his biceps were bulking up when he did simple motions like wringing his shirt out. I started to think about how big they would be when he was truly flexing. I didn't realize I was staring until he started chuckling.

"What are you looking at?"

I could feel myself blushing and I turned away. "Nothing, sorry."

Suddenly he was gone. A few seconds later, I felt him take my hand, and pull me forward and up. The next thing I knew, I was in some type of cave. It was small, but it was dry and warm.

I looked over at Bryan. "How did you find this?"

He shrugged as he sat down. "My dad taught me how to play the guitar when I was younger and we used to search the woods for a place where we could spend time together and play our guitars. It was something we both had a passion for. Unfortunately, we never found that special place and then my dad died. I continued to look for a place that would remind me of him and where I could play my guitar in peace. Then one day, I was messing around in the waterfall and found this cave."

"I'm so sorry, Bryan."

He wiped the tears from his eyes and looked down at the ground saying, "Don't worry about it. It was a couple of years ago. My dad used to tell me that whenever I played, he would hear the music that filled the room. So I never play half-heartedly. I don't want to disappoint him."

Bryan stood up and walked to the cave entrance. I walked over and leaned against the wall next to him. As I did that, I looked over at him only to find that he was looking intently down at me. I smiled slightly as he put one of his hands on my waist and gently moved a strand of my hair with the other hand. He reached up to place his hand on my cheek and then leaned in to kiss me. This time, I didn't object. Instead, I stretched up to meet his lips. At first he kissed me softly, but then he started kissing me deeper. His lips were warm on mine. I smiled when he pulled away and wrapped his arms around me, pulling me against his chest. I hadn't even thought about Chase. I was here and this guy had my attention. He was what I had been looking for, someone I could confide in. There was something about Chase that I couldn't quite forget about, but for right now, in this moment with Bryan, it felt right being there in his arms.

CHAPTER 8

The next morning I woke up with a huge smile on my face. Even after I remembered that my dad was getting married to the wicked witch of the east, I was still smiling. I owed it all to Bryan. Even though we had only spent one day together, I felt like I could already trust him with my life.

I walked around my room aimlessly while getting dressed that morning. All the events that took place the day before were whirling through my mind. The waterfall, the mud, the song, the kiss. When I was decent, I walked downstairs only to find my dad and that wretched woman sitting at the dining room table. I could think of so many names I could call her; some of them being appropriate and others, not so much. I was about to sneak out of the house when my dad saw me.

"Katie! Can you come here a minute?" I walked in there with my eyes locked on my dad, not wanting to see her.

"What's up, Dad?" I looked down and saw open binders on the table and realized they were planning the wedding.

"Well, Carrie has something to tell you. I think it would be best if she said it, not me." I knew what that meant; I had to look at her. It took all the energy in my body to peel my eyes off my dad and look at Carrie. I plastered a fake smile on my face, which in turn, was greeted by her fake smile.

"Katie, I just wanted to let you know that I'd like you to be one of my bridesmaids."

I felt my forced smile begin to fall apart. Before she could say anything more, I said, "I don't think so." I looked over at my dad who was frowning, and looked back over at Carrie. "What I meant was, I would be… honored." I started to think about all the things I would rather do than be her bridesmaid, like get attacked by a shark, cut off my ear, or get hit by a truck. But then my mind started to wander back to the waterfall and I began to smile. I snapped out of it when Carrie cleared her throat.

"That's what I thought. Anyway, what color do you think I should use for the bridesmaid's dresses? I'm thinking about teal, dark blue or baby blue. Which color do you like?"

I just looked at her and blurted out, "Are you depressed or are you just obsessed with blue? Isn't blue the color of sadness? Yet that is the only color you are thinking about letting your bridesmaid's wear—"

"Stop it!" Carrie stood up. "You are going to start treating me with respect. I am tired of you treating me like I am not worthy of your father! If you have a better idea, tell me. What color do you think I should pick?"

I glared at her. "What do I think? So all of a sudden you care about my opinion? Hmmm, let's see. How about black? It symbolizes death and destruction. Oh, and it's the color of your heart." I gave her a quick smirk before turning to walk out of the house. "And you aren't worthy of my dad, just in case you didn't know."

"Katie, that's enough! I don't want to hear another word from you, young lady!" My dad stood up as he was yelling at me. I grabbed my purse off the table in the hall and walked out of the house and to my car. When I was inside my car with the doors locked, I leaned back against the seat and took a deep breath. I couldn't believe what I had just done, but I wasn't sorry. If anything, I was happy I did it. Something wasn't right about her. I started my car and saw that it was noon. I drove over to the nearest Subway to get a sandwich.

When I finished my lunch, I started to walk out of the restaurant when I got an idea. I walked back up to the cashier and ordered another sandwich. When I had paid for it, I walked out to my car and drove to the only horse ranch I could remember. When I turned onto the dusty road, I started to speed up, already wishing I was there. I got to the driveway, which if you ask me wasn't much of a driveway. It was like driving on a trail in the woods. After I parked and turned the car off, I sat there staring at what was in front of me. There was a white brick building, which from the looks of it had a first and second level. Off to the side of the building was a huge red barn. The barn's two wide doors were open to reveal dozens of horse stalls. Then to the right of the barn, there was a horse corral. I opened my door to get out of my car when I remembered the first time Lucas ever rode a horse.

"I can't believe I let you talk me into this…" Lucas smiled over at me as he put his riding helmet on. I chuckled as I continued to get the knots out of the mane of the horse that Lucas would be riding.

"This is the reason you came to summer camp, to have new experiences. So have a new experience." I glanced over at him and smiled.

Before I knew it, I felt his hands wrap around my waist from behind me. "No, the reason I came to summer camp was to spend more time with you." He leaned down and kissed the side of my neck. I gently turned around in his arms to face him.

"But as a bonus, you get to ride a horse." I put my hand on the back of his head and pulled his head down until his lips met mine.

It was the summer after our freshman year and we had now been dating for seven months. Our parents weren't going to let us go to the same camp at first, but we talked them into it. We both repeated over and over that we were good kids and they should just trust us and then they did. Lucas pulled away from me when his riding instructor rounded the corner.

When he saw Lucas and I standing there he said, "Lucas, what are you doing? The rest of the group is already on the trail! Don't worry. Your girlfriend will be here when you get back." Lucas chuckled and quickly got on top of the horse. Greg, the instructor, reached into a bucket on the ground, pulled out a carrot and fed it to the horse.

"Now Lucas, you're riding Moonlight. She is one of the best, hardworking horses we have, so you should be fine. Now get out on the trail and attempt to find the group, please!" Lucas looked over and winked at me before riding out of the barn.

I sighed as the memory of Lucas faded. I climbed out of my car, putting my phone and keys in my back pocket. I walked inside the building and went to the front desk. There was a teenager about my age behind it. She was blonde with blue eyes. Her nametag identified her as Rachel and I smiled as I walked up to her.

"Hey. Um…Rachel. Do you know where Bryan is?"

She looked up at me and responded, "That depends on who's asking."

I looked at her. Where did her attitude come from? I lifted up my Subway bag. "I have his lunch." She nodded and pointed to the horse stable. I shook my head as I walked out the door and looked out into the huge stable. There were at least 30 or more stalls by the smell of it.

I started walking down the long row of horse stalls

until I saw a familiar black cowboy hat. It was Bryan. He was talking to a little girl, probably around 3 or 4 years of age, and her mom about a horse. He kept pointing to the horse then would answer a couple of questions. I smiled as I started to walk over to him. I tapped him on the shoulder and he turned around. When he saw me, his eyes lit up and a big smile appeared on his face. He turned to the child's mother and said "Okay, if you have any more questions, just call me." Then he looked down at the little girl, leaned over and put his hands on his knees and said "Good riding today, Michelle. I'll see you next week."

Bryan lifted up his hand and the little girl gave him a high five. When he stood up, she tugged on his hand. He looked down, smiled and asked, "Yes?" She reached up with her hands and said, "Hug." I couldn't help but smile when he reached down and hugged her, and then picked her up and twirled her around. When he set her down, he laughed. "See y'all. Bye, Michelle. Bye, Nina." He tilted his hat to Nina. When they walked away, he turned to me and wrapped me in his arms. He kissed me lightly. "This is a nice surprise. What are you doing here?"

I lifted up the Subway bag and smiled. "I figured you would get hungry soon, so I decided I would bring you some food."

He smiled and nodded. "I'm starving. Come on. We'll eat in my truck." He grabbed the hand that didn't have the food in it and smiled down at me. When he walked back inside the building, he held the door open for me and led me through. When we were around the receptionist's desk, he turned to me and took my sunglasses off my face and put them on.

"How do I look? I think this is my style." He chuckled, and I looked over at Rachel who was glaring at me.

I looked up at him and laughed. "They may not be your best look." I smiled again as I took them back and put them on.

He sighed and mumbled, "Dang it, I really thought I looked good." He laughed. When we walked past Rachel, Bryan looked back at her. "Hey Rachel, I'm going on my lunch break." She just smiled at him and nodded.

I let Bryan lead me out of the building and to his truck. As usual, he opened the passenger door for me before walking over to his side. He had one of those trucks where the front seat went all the way across, which made it one big seat. So when he got in, I scooted over so I could sit by him. He put his arm around me and ate with one hand. I smiled over at him.

"This is really good." He laughed and I looked down at my hands. He wrapped his food up and set it on the dashboard. "Is anything bothering you?"

I looked over at him. "Bryan, there is something I need to tell you. I need to tell someone and I want it to be you. I haven't told anyone the whole story yet." He just nodded, so I knew he understood. "It's about one of my boyfriends."

"Oh, the one that died." I looked over at him confused.

"How did you know?"

He smiled over at me. "Katie, it's a small town. When your dad told his poker buddies, the word kind of got around." He shrugged.

"But if you knew, why didn't you say anything?"

He looked over at me. "If you wanted to talk about it, I figured that you would tell me when you were ready. I wasn't going to rush you."

I stretched up and kissed his cheek. "Thank you. But I really want to tell you what happened from my point of view. I've never told anyone how much it impacted me." He nodded as I looked out the front window and took a deep breath.

"It was late, almost his curfew. He wanted to do something I wasn't ready for. So I made him leave. I guess he was rushing home and lost control of the car." I started to get teary eyed when Bryan reached over to rub my back.

"His death had nothing to do with you."

I shook my head. "It had everything to do with me. If I had put my foot down and made him leave when he needed to, he would have had plenty of time to get home. He might not have rushed." I paused for a second to calm down. "When he was on his way home, the roads were wet. I was starting to get worried about Lucas, so I texted him. The officers said his phone was open to my message. My text message. If I had waited, he wouldn't have gotten distracted." I covered my face with my hands and Bryan pulled me closer to his side.

"You didn't mean to. You didn't know." I laid my head down on his shoulder and started crying.

"I feel so bad all the time. It's my fault and I can't forget that. Everywhere I go, everyone I see, brings back the memory of him. No matter what I do to try to forget, I always remember. It's like someone is constantly saying, 'How can you be happy, when Lucas is dead.' But when I'm with you, it's like I can get through it. I don't have that ache anymore."

I looked up at him. "Thanks for listening. I owe you one." I smiled and leaned up to kiss him again. After a few seconds he pulled away.

"I think we're even. This sandwich counts for more than anything I've ever done for you."

I began to notice what he was wearing. A white shirt, unbuttoned halfway down with the sleeves rolled to his elbows, a black muscle shirt underneath and black cowboy boots with spurs.

I couldn't resist teasing him. "Bryan, you're starting to look like a cowboy."

He laughed. "Well, I guess that's a good thing." He looked at me intently.

After a second I asked, "What?"

"When my dad died, I thought I was worthless and I thought nobody could ever love me. But then you came along. Nobody has ever made me feel like you do, Katie." He leaned down to kiss me. When our lips finally parted, I smiled and rested my head on his chest while his arms wrapped around me. I could feel his chest moving up and down, and I could hear him breathe.

I finally broke the silence by saying, "Well, I guess we saved each other."

He chuckled. "Yes, we did." I felt him kiss the top of my head.

"You know what we're doing tonight?" I asked him.

"No. What are we doing?"

"It's time for you to meet my dad."

He groaned, but it turned into a laugh. "I already know him."

I just shook my head. "I meant introduce you as my boyfriend." I could almost see the smile that I felt sure was on his lips.

"Sounds good." I smiled at that and wrapped my arms around him. I turned my head and kissed his chest. This would definitely be a surprise for my dad, but I was happy I had Bryan to lean on. Knowing that no matter what I go through, he'll always be there, holding my hand and pushing me forward.

For the rest of the day, I watched Bryan give little kids riding lessons, and it wasn't until we were walking to the truck that I started to get nervous. I knew my dad would like Bryan, but this would only be the second guy my dad has met. The first one was Lucas, and at first my dad didn't like him very much, but he warmed up to him. I just hope Bryan wouldn't have to wait awhile. Of course, my dad already knew who he was, but he didn't know Bryan as my boyfriend. When I climbed into the truck, I scooted over beside Bryan as he rested his arm behind me on the seat.

When he pulled out of the parking lot, I mumbled, "Are you nervous?"

I looked hesitantly over at him as he looked at me from the corner of his eye and shook his head. "No. He already knows me. I'll just be something different to him now." He shrugged and smiled.

We drove in silence the rest of the way to the house. I only spoke when I was giving him directions.

When we got past the front gate, Bryan broke the silence. "Dang. My whole house could probably fit in your kitchen." He laughed. His laugh was contagious, so when he started laughing, so did I. We pulled up to the driveway and as he stopped the truck, I saw my dad walk out to greet us. I started to open the door, but noticed Bryan was coming around to open the door for me. I thanked him as he helped me down.

My dad walked up to us and greeted Bryan. "Hey, Bryan. I didn't expect to see you here."

I looked over at my dad and was about to say something when Bryan said, "Yes, sir. I didn't expect to be here tonight either, sir." He smiled at my dad. When he did, I could feel the tension disappear from my dad. So Bryan had that effect on everyone, not just me.

"Dad, I have something I need to tell you." My dad looked at me then looked away when Carrie called his name. I groaned, "Dad, it's important!"

He looked over at me and nodded. "What is it? Maybe we should go talk inside if it's private."

I shook my head. "No. It involves Bryan."

My dad nodded. "Okay, well, we can talk about this later, alright? Carrie is calling me."

I grabbed his hand before he walked away. "Bryan is my boyfriend. I thought you should know because you're going to be seeing a lot of him."

My dad turned around and looked at me. "What did you just say? Katie, if this is some kind of plan to forget about Lucas, don't use Bryan like that."

I shook my head. "Dad, I really like Bryan. It has nothing to do with Lucas! Just go inside, Carrie's calling you." The idea finally sunk into me, I might be losing my dad. It seemed the past couple of days he hung on every word she said; and every time she called, he would drop everything to go see if she needed help... even if he was helping me. My dad just looked at me with pain in his eyes, as if he was contemplating what he should do. He sighed before turning to walk away. My eyes started to tear up and automatically I hid my face in Bryan's chest. When his arms wrapped around me, I started to feel better.

"I feel so insignificant when she is around. Like all he notices is her. I don't even know who he is anymore."

Bryan started to rub my back and sighed. "I don't know what you're going through, but I can imagine how that feels." He kissed the top of my head while I wiped my eyes.

"Well, I better get inside, and you better get home." He nodded and smiled down at me before he leaned down to kiss me gently.

I said, "Goodnight. Drive safely." And then waved to him as he got in his truck. "Wait! My car is still at the stables."

Bryan smiled. "I'll swing by tomorrow morning and we can go pick it up together."

I watched him drive down the road before walking inside the house. I walked straight up to my room and changed into sweatpants and a T-shirt. I was about to fall asleep when I heard my door open. I squinted my eyes against the light and could see that it was my dad. I sat up and leaned against the head of the bed as he sat at the foot of it.

"Katie, do you really think a boyfriend is what you need right now?"

I looked at him. "What do you mean by right now? Nothing is going on right now. I like him. A lot."

My dad looked over at me with gentle eyes. "But you're leaving in a couple days. When are you going to see him?"

I felt a smile sneak onto my face. "I'm going to be coming here a lot, remember? I'm a bridesmaid. I have to help plan the wedding."

He looked at me and shook his head. "What do you have against her? You don't even know her."

I asked sarcastically, "Why would I want to get to know her? I walked in the door and could tell she was a fake. Maybe she isn't, but why would I want to subject myself to that?"

"Promise me you'll try to give her a chance." My dad looked at me sternly, so I nodded.

"I do have one question, Dad. You like Bryan, so why don't you want us dating?" I looked up at him.

"I don't want to see you get hurt again. If something were to happen to him, you would be crushed. If what happened to Lucas were to happen again, I don't think you would recover this time. When you got hurt, you closed everyone off. You wouldn't eat, you wouldn't drink. I don't want to see you go through that again."

"Okay. I get where you're coming from, but why can't you just be supportive?"

He sighed and smiled, "I love the kid, Katie, and I'm glad it's him and not some pothead teenager. Now get some sleep. Tomorrow you're going to get your bridesmaid's dress."

I chuckled and mumbled, "The black one?"

He smiled and kissed me on the forehead. "Goodnight, Katie. I love you."

"Night Dad." I pulled the covers over my head and closed my eyes.

CHAPTER 9

The next morning when we pulled into the little parking lot where the dress shop was located, I sighed. I already wanted this day to be over. The dress shop was a cozy little place. It sat between a diner and an antique store. It was made out of white wood with an oversized brown door. The store also had two big windows that let lots of light into it. The windows had two elegant white drapes that hung from the top of them, each held back by golden tassels.

When Carrie parked the car, she got out and waited on the sidewalk for me. I really wish someone could have come with us...anyone. I just didn't want to be here alone with her. As I climbed out of the car, I saw that she was tapping her foot with impatience. She was wearing a very short, revealing bright red dress with sunglasses that took up half of her already small face. I walked past her into the store and I heard her sigh.

When we got inside, I followed her over to the counter where a plump older lady was sitting in a chair. She had gray hair with brown eyes. I smiled at her before I turned to look around the room. When you walked inside the store, the first thing you noticed was the spotless white carpet. Past the foyer, two steps led down into the main area which contained two large leather couches for customer seating. Behind them and against the wall, were two racks of dresses. There were more clothes racks scattered around the room.

Carrie's voice suddenly filled the quiet store. "Hello, Joyce. I'm here to pick up the bridesmaid's dresses, but we need to get one hemmed for Katie." She nodded at me, then looked back over at Joyce. "And I need to get my wedding dress hemmed, too."

Joyce nodded and went over to a clothes rack and took down a couple of light blue dresses. When she brought them over to the counter, she said, "Here are the bridesmaid's dresses."

I shook my head. "That's not right. The brides-maids' dresses are black." When I said that, Carrie grabbed my arm.

Carrie quickly looked at Joyce as she said, "Excuse us." Then she turned back to me and pushed me behind a rack of clothes. She looked down at me as she said, "Look, I don't want you to be in my wedding anymore than you want to be in it. But I'm doing it for your father, so you need to cool it. I love your father, so you need to step back and see that he isn't just yours anymore."

I shook my head. "Shut up. You're a fake. I can see it, and my dad will soon. So don't bother putting on a show for me."

Carrie gasped, "You know what? With that atti-tude, I no longer need you as a bridesmaid. You can leave." Then she turned and walked back to the coun-ter, saying to Joyce, "I'll go to the back and try on my wedding dress so you can hem it." Joyce nodded and walked back to the dressing room with Carrie.

I sighed and took out my phone. I sent a simple text message to Bryan with two words, "help me." I clicked on his name then slid my phone into my pocket. I walked back to the dressing rooms and sat down on a couch. A short time later, a clerk from the front poked her head behind the curtain.

"Miss, someone is out front for you." I started to wonder who it could be as I walked to the front. People's names started to run through my mind, but I knew who I wanted to it be. When I got to the front of the store, I could feel my face light up when I saw Bryan standing there. He was wearing brown Cargo shorts with a red, short sleeve shirt that said 'lifeguard' in big white letters. He was also wearing brown leather flip flops. My eyes went back up to his shirt as a vision of Lucas appeared in my mind. It was the summer before junior year and Lucas' best friend was lifeguarding at one of the local pools. Lucas and I would always go to that pool on the day his best friend was working because he let us do whatever we wanted.

"Your turn." Lucas said as he climbed out of the water and walked over to the diving board that I was now standing on the edge of. I looked down at the water.

"I can't do it. I've never done a flip off a diving board." Lucas walked up behind me on the diving board and slid his arms around my waist as he whispered in my ear.

"It's easy. You do flips all the time in the grass and on my trampoline. It's the same thing. You're just going to land in the water." All of a sudden, I heard a loud whistle coming from the lifeguard stand and then Hunter, Lucas' best friend, yelled "Everyone clear the water!" Then he dove in. I looked around and noticed an old man floating face down near the deep end of the pool. He looked like he was probably over 200 pounds. Hunter was swimming over to him and then flung the man's arm around his neck.

I heard a second splash and saw Lucas swimming over to help his friend. Lucas got on the opposite side of the man and flung the other arm over his shoulders. Together, Lucas and Hunter guided the man to the edge of the pool.

I quickly blinked my eyes to get my thoughts away from Lucas. Bryan was now walking towards me asking, "Hey, you okay?"

"Yeah, I'm just tired of being here." Before he could protest, I buried my face in his chest as I held on to him.

"Come on."

I froze and looked up at him. "What?"

He chuckled and said, "I'm bailing you out." I started laughing and let him lead me out of the store and to his truck. When we got in his truck, he handed me a bandana and quickly said, "Put that on." I looked over at him with a confused look on my face and he smiled. "Trust me." He grabbed the bandana and put it over my eyes. I don't really know how long we drove, but soon the road got bumpy, so I guessed Bryan was on a back road.

"Where are you taking me?"

He laughed and said, "Shhh. We're almost there."

Suddenly, his truck made a sharp turn and then started backing up. I really wanted to see what we were doing. I was about to say something when Bryan cut off the engine, and leaned over and kissed me. His lips were soft and warm, and I smiled. He gently slid off the bandana and I looked at him.

"Where are we?"

He smiled at me. "I have to get something set up, so promise me you won't turn around." I nodded. I wrapped one arm around his neck and put the other behind his head and intertwined my fingers in his hair and kissed him. A couple seconds later, he chuckled and pulled away. "I'll be right back. Don't turn around." He gave me a quick peck and got out of the car. I really wanted to turn around and see what he was doing, but I didn't. I faced forward and saw the dirt road we must have come in on. It was lined closely by dense, green woods. I saw two squirrels on one of the trees. As they chased each other around, I smiled. I heard a lot of movement in the back of Bryan's truck and was about to peak when suddenly he was on my side of the truck and opened the door for me. He helped me out and covered my eyes with his hands. We walked a couple of feet, and then he stopped and removed his hands. I gasped in amazement when I saw that we were on the edge of a huge lake. I smiled at the ducks swimming around.

"Bryan, this is absolutely amazing!" I looked at him and he smiled.

"This isn't all of it." He placed his hands on my shoulders and spun me around to face the bed of his truck. My jaw was probably on the ground as I stared at a picnic blanket spread out in the back of his truck with a few lighted candles on the edges of the truck, even though it was broad daylight. There was a dark brown picnic basket in the middle of it all, and his guitar on top of his tool box.

I looked at Bryan in astonishment. "What is this?"

He smiled and looked down at me with his green eyes sparkling in the sun. Bryan responded, "I wanted to arrange something special for you."

"How long have you been planning this?"

"Well, when you texted me, I thought you needed to get away from everything. I remembered how you said you always wanted a picnic on the beach. But this is as close to a beach as we have." He shrugged and smiled.

"You're really something else." I smiled and stretched up on my toes to give him a kiss.

He wrapped his arms around my waist and mumbled against my lips, "I love you."

I froze and pulled away. Last time a guy told me that I screwed up and didn't tell him how I felt. I can't change that moment, but this moment I can control. This time, I wasn't going to regret holding my words back.

I looked up at Bryan and smiled. "I love you, too."

Bryan lifted me up into his truck and then climbed in after me. I crawled to the front of the truck bed and leaned against the cab. Bryan sat right next to me and put his arm around my shoulders for a brief hug. Releasing me, he pulled the basket on his lap and pulled out two sandwiches, a salad, fruit, and a plate full of cookies. Finally, he pulled out two water bottles.

I looked over at him and smiled my thanks. Suddenly, I didn't want to go back to my mom's house. I wanted to stay right here in this moment with Bryan. I wanted to stay with him, period. But I knew that wasn't an option, because unfortunately, I had school on Monday. I guess he could tell something was wrong because he looked over at me and asked, "What? Did I forget something? I knew I should have brought chips."

I laughed and rested my head on his shoulder. "No, everything is perfect. Thank you." I kissed the side of his neck.

"Then what is it?"

I sighed and said, "I don't want to go home tomorrow. I'm going to miss you too much."

He chuckled. "Well, you know where to find me. I'll always be here for you, if you need somewhere to run. I won't let you down." I smiled as he said that. We sat there for a few seconds and then he said, "I want to share something with you." He suddenly sat up and grabbed his guitar. He moved to sit on the edge of the truck. "I wrote a song." He started to strum the guitar and sing.

"Maybe it's too good to say; maybe it's too soon to see,

But it may not matter as long as we trust,

But it's too big of a step for a ring on the hand,

Maybe we just want to be free, to have wings like an eagle,

So beautiful and free, fly anywhere we want to be,

Wings like an eagle,

We came so long in a day,

So many words to say,

Not enough breath in the day,

Wings like an eagle so beautiful and free,

Go anywhere we want to be,

Just as long as you're there with me."

He kept strumming for a little bit, then stopped and looked at me.

"It's usually hard for me to talk about my feelings. I find it easier to say them in a song. You're different, Katie. I can't see myself without you anymore." He laid his guitar down, crawled over beside me and then cradled my face in his hands to kiss me. When he pulled away, he sat down beside me again and I looked over at him.

"I loved it. Thank you for writing me a song." I smiled and laid my head on his shoulder, and we just sat there enjoying being together.

As the sun was setting a few hours later, Bryan sighed before saying, "I should take you to the stables so you can pick up your car."

I nodded reluctantly before climbing out of the back of his truck. He followed my lead and climbed into the front seat, before backing out and heading towards the stables.

CHAPTER 10

The following Monday I woke up to the sound of a car honking in my driveway. I groaned and pulled myself out of bed and went over to the window seeing Chase in his car. I smiled and waved before closing my curtains. I looked over at the clock and saw that it was 8:30. I was late for school on the first day back. Quickly changing into some shorts and a T-shirt, I walked outside with only my phone. Chase got out of his Hummer to come hug me. When I pulled away from the hug, I looked down and saw that he was in faded blue jeans and a hot pink Nike shirt that said 'Just do It' in big white letters. He was wearing a white hat and of course, his white vans. I was starting to wonder if he had any other shoes.

He smiled at me and said, "Well, let's get going." He elbowed me, then walked over to his car and climbed into his seat. As I walked over to the passenger side, I started to think about Bryan. Maybe opening the door for people wasn't part of southern hospitality. It was just something Bryan did. I was smiling just thinking about him. Suddenly, I couldn't wait for it to be Friday. As I closed my door, Chase put the car in drive and started to back out of my driveway and head out of the neighborhood. There were a couple of minutes of silence before we drove into a big parking lot. I looked out and saw a carnival.

I looked over at Chase and smiled. "We're skipping school for the county fair?"

I laughed when he interrupted and said, "Hey! This is a very important fair. There is a lot of value coming here. And—"

He stopped talking and chuckled. "So what? We skipped school for a county fair. Since you were gone all spring break, I wanted to go somewhere with you and have fun before we got back into the school schedule."

I looked over at him. "Aw, that's sweet, but we hang out every day after school. I don't think the school schedule messes us up that bad." He shrugged and smiled. All of a sudden, he jumped out of the car and waited patiently for me to get out. I walked over to him and nudged him lightly. As we started walking, I began to hear the music playing in the speakers. We walked past the building where you buy your tickets and I looked over at Chase. "Where are we going?"

Chase smiled, "My uncle is on the committee for the fair so we get in free."

I rolled my eyes. "Is there anything your family doesn't do?"

He shook his head and chuckled, "No, not really." He looked down at the ground. "Just kidding. My family likes to be involved with the community." He shrugged like it was no big deal. I shook my head as I kept looking forward so I didn't trip over any of the cords or little kids. We walked past all the rides and found a large enclosed netted area. I heard things being shot and saw big wooden structures before I actually saw the people inside. I looked over at Chase, confused. As a big smile spread across his face, he said, "I'm going to teach you how to paintball." I laughed like he was joking, but I could tell he was serious so I stopped laughing.

"Wait, you're serious. Wow, I think you really just want me to get killed." He laughed and pulled me inside a wooden building. He walked over to the rack where the guns and the 'armor' were. I shook my head; guys took things WAY too seriously. I chuckled as I slid the vest on. Chase quickly showed me how to use the gun and what to do if I wanted out. I thought I had it all down, so I slid my facemask on and walked outside into the netted area.

The officials had paused the shooting for us so we walked in and got into position on our side. I sighed in relief that Chase was on my side because number one, I didn't want to be by myself with boys I didn't know; and number two, he looked like he played a lot so I'm pretty sure he knows what he is doing. When the whistle blew everyone started to shoot, and all around me, everyone's clothes turned the color of the paint. All the wooden structures that surrounded me began to take on the color of a rainbow. I grunted lightly when I got hit in the knee, twice. I looked down and saw two big blotches of color. They wanted to play that way, fine. Two people could play that way, even if I was a girl. I smiled as I shot my gun and hit someone square in the chest.

I don't know how long we played, but when the ref blew the whistle signaling that the other team was out, I smiled. I slid off my facemask and went to shake all of the guy's hands. I didn't realize how sweaty or colorful I was until I slid off the little vest. I looked over at Chase as he was sliding off his facemask. In place of his white hat was now a hat with an array of different colors. I laughed. He came over and hugged me, lifting me up in the air and making my fairly clean shirt stained with all the colors on his shirt. When he set me down, he kept looking at me. I looked up at him and smiled.

Suddenly, out of nowhere, he put his hands on each side of my face and leaned down and kissed me. I pushed away as hard as I could. When he let go, I couldn't look at him. I threw my gun, vest, and facemask on the ground and ran out of the netted area. I could feel the tears filling my eyes. I started to run as fast as I could into the woods by the fair. When I was really deep in, I leaned against a tree and cried.

Why was I crying? Some part of me didn't want him to stop kissing me, that part of me wanted Chase. But a bigger part yearned for Bryan. I slid down the tree to the ground and buried my face in my hands. What was happening to me? I couldn't love Chase;

he was my best friend, my brother. It would ruin everything good that was going for me. Why were these feelings coming to the surface now? What if they were always there? What if I had always felt this way about Chase, but the loss of Lucas covered it up?

But ever since I met Bryan, I felt that weight lifted off my shoulders. Lucas wasn't a burden anymore. So now that the shadow covering my feelings had been lifted, I was seeing clearly. But why were my feelings this strong? Sure, Chase and I had something special. Sure, I trusted him with everything I was. But this was too much for me to handle. This was something I had to work out by myself because I couldn't talk to Chase about it, and I certainly couldn't talk to Bryan. I was at loss with myself, with Chase, with Bryan, and it seemed like lately, I had been at a loss with the world.

Suddenly there was noise in the brush beside me. I quickly wiped my tears away and looked up to see Chase standing there still covered in paint.

"How did you find me?"

He smiled my smile. "Well, it wasn't that hard. You left a paint trail, and then when the trail stopped, all the yellow that's on you made you stick out like a sore thumb." He chuckled and came to sit down beside me and took a deep breath. "I'm sorry, I shouldn't have done that."

I shook my head, "No, it was me. I overreacted. I don't know what came over me."

He nodded. "Well, let's just talk about something else." He smiled at me. "What are your plans for the summer?"

I shrugged. "I think I'm going to go up to my dad's a lot this summer, just to get out of town. I have someone to hang out with up there, so I'm not completely alone with my dad and his soon-to-be-wife." I shuddered when I started thinking about Carrie. When I looked over at Chase, he was smirking.

"Well, I'm glad you have a friend over there, but I don't know what I'm going to do without you this summer." He smiled. "Just kidding. I'm actually applying for a job at the Nike outlet store, so hopefully they give me a lot of hours."

I snuck a glance at Chase and smiled. He always seemed to say the right thing that ended up calming me down. I knew why I felt the way I did about him. The more I thought about it, there was nothing not to like about Chase. I started to see why the girls picked him. He was great. It was almost like he never tried, that's just how he was. As I started to think about Chase, my mind switched to Bryan. I couldn't go a minute without him popping into my mind.

As we sat there in silence just looking out into the trees, I started to subconsciously compare Bryan and Chase. The more I thought about it, they were alike; but at the same time, they were completely different. I leaned my head against the back of the tree and surrendered. I give up. I needed both of them. I just needed to find out which one I wanted the most, because it wouldn't be right to have both, even though that thought crossed my mind.

CHAPTER 11

The next day was torture. Not only did I have homework for skipping school, but knowing how I felt about Chase made it hard to just be friends with him. This weekend, I would have to do a lot of thinking. I knew I had to think about what I wanted, and fast. Before it becomes harder and harder, and before I fall deeper in love with both of them.

As I pulled up to the house after school, I slowly climbed out of my car. My parents weren't home yet, so I had the quiet house to just think. I went up to my room and fell down on my bed. I sighed as I rolled over facing the ceiling. My eyelids closed over my eyes and everything went black.

I was only asleep for about 10 minutes before someone rang the doorbell. I sighed as I heaved myself off my bed and walked downstairs to the door. I unlocked the door and opened it. The one person I wasn't expecting to see was on my front porch.

"Bryan? What are you doing here?" He was wearing his leather cross necklace with his purple jacket zipped up halfway, revealing a black v-neck shirt, faded blue jeans and his usual white vans.

He smiled as he said, "I couldn't wait for this weekend. It's so boring up there now that you're gone." He shrugged and chuckled. "So are you going to make me stay out here all evening?"

I laughed. "Be patient. I was getting there." I opened the door all the way for him and grabbed his hand as he walked in. We walked upstairs to my room. I crawled on my bed and leaned against the headboard. I watched as Bryan walked over to the rocking chair that sat in the corner of my room. It had been there idle for the past couple of months. As he sat down in it, I smiled at him. But then all of a sudden, a picture of Lucas sitting in the chair flashed in front of my eyes and as it stayed there, Lucas opened his mouth and said, "You're forgetting me, and you don't care. When it's your fault I'm dead." I gasped and quickly covered my eyes. Within a second, I could feel arms around me.

"Katie! What happened?" Bryan's voice was right by my ear and I shuddered into his chest.

"It's my fault. I couldn't save him. I should have made him leave earlier..." I started to cry. Bryan didn't say anything; he didn't have to. He sat there with me while I cried it out. He continued to rub my back in a circular motion while holding me against his chest. After I was done crying, I wiped my eyes with my hand, then pulled them away from my face. "I'm sorry."

He shook his head and kissed my forehead. "Don't worry about it. What happened?"

I looked down at my lap and answered, "Lucas...I saw him." I looked over at my rocking chair through the corner of my eye, then quickly hid my face in Bryan's chest. He sighed and put his hand on the back of my head.

"It's okay, I'm here." I looked up at Bryan, who was looking at the chair. "I hate how it haunts you." I looked down at my lap and laid my head down on his chest.

He said, "Let's talk about something else."

"Like what?"

"Tell me something that you've always wanted to do."

I shifted my weight, "I don't know. Um...Let me think. Does it have to be in a certain category?"

He laughed. "Come on, just pick something."

I thought for a second before saying, "I've always wanted to feel like I'm flying in the rain." I looked up at Bryan when he didn't answer. He looked like he was deep in thought. After a couple of seconds, he got a big smile on his face and looked down at me.

"Let's go. I want to take you somewhere." I smiled and nodded. I didn't care where he was taking me, as long as I was with him. We walked downstairs hand in hand and then out to his car. When we got to the passenger side door, he opened the door for me. I smiled as I hopped in his truck. I scooted over beside him when he started driving and felt his right arm behind me against the seat. I laid my head on his shoulder and yawned. I looked up at him as he chuckled and said, "You can take a nap if you want to. I'll wake you up when we get there."

I shook my head. "No, I'm okay." But a few minutes later, I was out. I was certain I felt someone kiss my forehead and move my bangs out of my face before I fell asleep.

I thought it was part of a dream until I heard Bryan say, "Katie. Wake up. We're here."

I opened my eyes and there was Bryan smiling down at me with gentle, understanding eyes. I looked in front of us and there was a little house. It was made out of light brown wood with oversized, double wooden front doors, and on the roof it had one of those old stone chimneys. I couldn't help but smile at the sight. The landscaping was beautiful. There were pine trees in front and surrounding the walkway leading to the door, there were bushes with little red and purple flowers.

"Where are we?"

"My uncle's house and it's Tuesday, which means his family doesn't get home until later."

"Why are we here?" Bryan didn't answer. Instead he got a bright smile on his face and led me inside the house. As we walked inside, the smell of baking cookies drifted over us. I heard footsteps and was trying to figure out where they were coming from when I saw a man walk around a corner. He was wearing denim shorts and a red polo shirt. He looked at Bryan and immediately smiled.

"Bryan. What a surprise. I never thought you would

drop by." He walked over and hugged him, then looked down at me. "Who is this young lady?"

Bryan cleared his throat, "This is Katie. Katie, this is my uncle, Lance." Lance nodded and reached for my hand. When I put my hand in his, he shook it and then let it go.

He smiled down at me. "Well, Bryan, you couldn't have picked a prettier one."

Bryan nodded. "I don't think I really picked her, it just happened." I smiled as Bryan talked. "Well, I'm going to show her the back."

Lance said, "Feel free to use anything out there."

Bryan smiled and pulled me to the back door. When he opened it for me, I noticed we weren't just at any house…this was a lake house. I smiled and looked over at him. "Don't say anything until you see it all." He laughed as he walked me over to the boat dock. There was something covered by a tarp. Bryan let go of my hand and grabbed the tarp and pulled it off, revealing two jet skis. I looked over at him.

"Bryan, what is all this?" He smiled.

"Well, it's not exactly raining, but I promise you'll feel like you're flying when you're on one of these babies…" he hit the front of one of the jet skis…"and it will feel like rain when the spray hits your face." I smiled and walked over to him.

"You're amazing." I kissed him and suddenly felt guilty. He gives me everything I want. I didn't deserve any of this, but I needed to be with Bryan. I had to feel his warmth, the way he hugged me made me feel wanted; like someone needed me. It felt like he was protecting me, watching over me.

"You okay?" He walked over to a lever and held it down. As he did that, the jet skis started to lower down to the water.

"Yeah, I'm fine. Do you come here a lot?"

Bryan shook his head. "I did when my dad was alive, but now my mom won't come within a 10-mile radius of this place. They still have a room here for me, you know, just in case." He looked out over the water and smiled.

When the jet skis were in the water, he let go of the lever and grabbed my shoulders to lead me down the ladder. At the bottom, he slid his vans off and when he did, I slid off my flip flops. I sat down on the purple Jet Ski and he sat down behind me.

"Since you don't know how to use them, I'm not going to let you ride it by yourself."

I nodded. "Good idea."

He leaned over me and unhooked something in the front of the Jet Ski. He quickly told me where the gas was and told me how to get started. I smiled as he wrapped his arms around my waist. I guessed to make sure if he fell off, I would, too. I slowly backed up the Jet Ski, then started forward. I understood now what he meant. The water flew past you, soaking you. I smiled because it did feel like I was flying in the rain. I couldn't believe it, only Bryan would think of a way to do this. It seemed like he always went out of his way to make me feel special.

All of a sudden a wave came out of nowhere and I pulled the gas down and the Jet Ski flipped. I flew into the water and was under for a couple of seconds before coming up. I laughed when I hit the surface.

I saw Bryan pop up and swim over to me. "You okay?"

I nodded. "I'm great." I wrapped my arms around his neck and smiled, "Don't worry."

I ran my hands through his wet hair and made it stick up in all directions. He swam us back over to the Jet Ski and got in front of me so he could drive back home. When he started it up, I wrapped my arms around his waist and rested my cheek against his back. The water was rushing past us. He must have been going twice the speed I had been going because we were home in about five minutes. He re-hooked the Jet Ski to the chain it had been attached to and helped me up the ladder. When we were both up, he wrapped me in his arms and kissed my collarbone. I reached up and wrapped my arms around his neck. He let go of me with one of his hands so he could pull the lever behind me. When the Jet Skis were in their berths, he placed the tarp back over them before reaching down and picking up both of our shoes.

We walked back into the house dripping wet and found two towels draped over a chair. Bryan took one for him and then gave me the other one. As we walked into the living area, I saw a blonde lady sitting with a girl a couple of years younger than us. I guessed one was Bryan's cousin and the other was his aunt.

The girl looked up and said, "Bryan!" She ran up to him and hugged him before pulling away and stretching out her hand to me. "I'm Claire and you must be Katie. My dad told me you were here." I smiled and shook her hand. I looked over at Claire's mom who was still staring at the TV and didn't even acknowledge Bryan.

I looked over at Bryan when he said, "Hello, Aunt Susie." His aunt turned her head and just stared at him; to me it looked more like a glare than a stare. I was confused. Bryan sighed and led me down a hallway to the farthest room. Inside there was a bed and that's it. I looked over at Bryan.

"What was wrong with her?" Bryan opened his closet door and pulled out a pair of sweatpants and shorts followed by two t-shirts.

"She's my dad's sister and she blames me for his death." He sighed and handed me the sweatpants and one of the shirts. "You can change in here."

"I have another question."

He nodded, "Okay, what is it?"

"You looked panicked when we flipped. Why?"

Bryan shook his head and answered, "It's not that I was panicked. If you don't remember, my dad died because our car flew into water. So of course I'm going to freak if stuff like that happens. And then I didn't see you come up." He smiled, bent down and kissed me. "I just can't lose you."

By the time I got home, it was almost midnight. The house lights were on and I was wondering why my parents were still up. I walked inside and was ambushed by Mike and my mom.

"Where were you?"

I looked over at them. "You don't have to wait around for me to get home. I'm not a kid anymore."

"Where were you?

"I was out with Chase. Sorry, we lost track of time."

"You were just with Chase?" Mike asked in a kind of skeptical way.

"Yes…"

"That's weird. He called around seven o'clock to see where you were." Mike crossed his arms.

"I was out with other friends. I'm really tired, so can I just go to bed?"

Mike nodded, and my mom asked, "What is going on with you?" She blocked the entrance to the stairs.

"I'm happy. Is that so bad?"

"You were happy with Lucas without breaking curfew," she said as she crossed her arms over her chest.

"Why do you bring up Lucas every time I do something you don't like? He isn't here. He's never coming back."

As that realization hit me, it felt as if a bomb had just exploded inside of me. For the first time since his death, it finally sunk in. Lucas is gone. I felt like I was going to throw up. I pulled my arms across my chest. I thought back to all the times Lucas had shown up in my moments with Chase and Bryan. He was always there in the back of my mind. I was tired of it. If he was gone and wasn't coming back, then I needed to let him go.

My mom snapped me back into reality as she said, "I know Lucas isn't here. I'm sorry. Just call us next time to tell us you're going to be late so we don't sit around worrying."

I nodded, walked upstairs and into my room. I walked over to the rocking chair and slid it out to my balcony and threw it over. I smiled when I heard it crash to the ground. From this day forth, I wouldn't let him stand in the way of me being happy. Not anymore.

CHAPTER 12

The next day at lunch, I sat down in my regular seat and waited for Chase to walk in. He wasn't hard to find, all I had to look for was a crowd of girls. I sighed and shook my head. But I stopped when I started to feel something I had never felt before when it came to Chase…I realized I was jealous. I wanted the girls to leave him alone. I wanted them to stop talking to him period. When he sat down next to me with that half smile on his face, I could feel myself turning red. He was wearing a light blue shirt with a bright red jacket that was zipped most of the way up. He had on dark blue jeans with red shoes that had blue Nike checks on the side of them.

Suddenly his smile turned to a frown. "Where were you yesterday? I went over to your house and your parents thought that you were with me."

I sighed and looked down. "I have other friends, you know? They kept bothering me to hang out with them." Chase made a sound with his lips. Like when you snap your tongue against the roof of your mouth.

"Katie, I know you have other friends. It was just a question. Did I offend you by walking in the door?"

I blurted out what I was thinking without meaning to say it. "You mean when you walked in with all those girls draped over you? Now why in the world would

I find that offensive? We aren't together, remember?"
Chase shook his head and walked out of the cafeteria.
I groaned and took out my phone to call Bryan. When
he picked up after the third ring, I smiled.

"Hey, sorry for calling. I just needed to hear your
voice."

"No, it's fine. This is my off period. What's up?"

I blurted out, "When can I meet your mom?" I
smacked myself in the head. I wasn't thinking before
I spoke today for some reason. He hesitated before
answering.

"I really want you to, but this isn't a very good time
for her right now. She's having a hard time control-
ling everything. Soon, okay?" I smiled and nodded, and
then the bell rang.

"Well, I have to go. I love you." Then I hung up. I
already felt better.

The rest of the day was a blur. As I drove home,
it finally hit me. Chase was mad at me. I didn't know
how I felt about that. When I pulled into my driveway,
I walked inside. I stared at the empty house. What was
I going to do now? With my best friend mad at me, I
didn't have anything to do. I sighed and knew what I
wanted, what I needed to do. I wrote a note to my
mom explaining that I was going out for a drive and I'd
be back later. Then I jogged back to my car. Why was I
in a hurry? I didn't know why, but I felt like I only had
a little window of time to do this in.

I drove to the highway then took the exit that went

to my dad's house. But instead of turning right on one of the winding roads, I kept driving. I remember Bryan had briefly told me where he lived. I pulled up to a little two story house that had no landscaping, with the blinds down on the windows. The house itself was made of dark brown wood. I remembered that Bryan said things were tight for him. That he paid for everything. I sighed as I parked my car. Suddenly, I wasn't sure if I should go in or even go to the door. I was fighting with myself. What if this wasn't his house? But then I saw his truck in the driveway. I knew I had to go talk to him at least. I drove all the way out here, so might as well. I slowly got out of the car.

When I walked to the front porch, I heard banging and Bryan yell, "Mom, don't touch that!" I was ready to turn around, but then my hand reached up and knocked. I heard Bryan call to his mom, "Mom stay here, and don't touch anything; I'm going to see who that is." I could hear him walking towards the door. I smiled as he opened the door. The first thing I noticed was his face. I guess he wasn't kidding when he said his mom was having a hard time. Because when she was having a hard time, she took it out on him. It looked like he hadn't shaved today so he had stubs all around his mouth, and along his sideburns. He was wearing a brown and grey button-down shirt that was halfway buttoned up with no undershirt. He had on grey pants that were tighter than what he usually wore, and green shoes. He was just staring at me while he leaned against the door. It looked like he was trying to take in that I was there.

"Wha... What are you doing here? Did you not understand that this isn't a good time?"

I took a step back. "I thought that you would be happy I'm here." I smiled a little bit, but his frown didn't budge.

"I am, but right now really isn't a good time." Right after he said that, a lady walked up. She had blonde hair that reached her shoulders. She was shorter than Bryan and was wearing green sweatpants with a pink shirt. She had a confused look on her face. She was holding a beer can.

"Bryan, why are you making this girl stand out in the cold? She must be freezing." It was April. It wasn't cold. I finally understood what Bryan meant. Not only was it hard for her to control her drinking, but it must have been hard for her mentally, too. She grabbed my arm roughly and dragged me in. When she talked, she took deep breaths in between each word, like she was deathly sick with some disease. Bryan sighed and moved out of the way so his mom could drag me in. When we were inside, I saw that to my right there was a living room. There was a big brown couch that was in the middle of the room and by the front window there was a small TV, which had newspapers all over it. On the wall hung a picture of Bryan, his mom, and a man. I assumed it was his dad. I smiled when I saw it. There was also a basket full of clothes. I wasn't sure if they were clean or dirty. In front of me there were stairs, then to the left there was a kitchen and in the middle of the kitchen there was a table with bottles of pills and beer bottles piled high. On the stove there was water boiling and in the sink there were dishes filled to the top. I looked over at Bryan who was staring at me with confusion; I guess as to why I was here.

"Katie, this is my mom, Julie." I went to shake her hand, but Julie looked at it confused. She touched my fingers, then turned and walked over to the kitchen. She stopped and shook her beer bottle.

"Bry, I need another beer. I'm out." She was still taking deep breaths between each word. I looked over at Bryan, who was shaking his head.

"Mom, you've had enough for today. It's time for water." His mom started shaking and she turned around and did something I wasn't expecting. She threw the bottle at him. I gasped and was relieved when he ducked out of the way just in time. Then Julie turned, walked into the kitchen and took a cup out of the sink. She pulled the boiling pot of water off the stove and was about to pour water into the cup and probably all over her hand, but out of the corner of my eye, I saw Bryan run over to her and yell, "Mom, no!" He grabbed her hand and pushed it out of the way, but couldn't get his hand out of the way before the boiling water ran all over it. He grunted and threw the pot of water into the sink. I ran over to him and started the cold water in the sink and put his hand under it. He pulled it away.

"I'm fine. You should not have come, Katie. I told you not to." He went over to his fridge and took out an ice pack and put it over his hand. "Do you ever listen to anyone?" He shook his head, then walked out the back door. I looked for his mom and sighed when I saw her sitting on the couch. She looked over at me.

"Don't go breaking my boy's heart now. He's been through enough." She was still breathing heavily and then she leaned her head back on the couch and fell asleep.

I turned back to the kitchen and started the water in the sink again. I cleaned the dishes until all of them were spotless. After that, I tried to put them all where they belonged, but I couldn't tell where some of them went. I looked into the backyard and saw Bryan sitting in a white boat with a blue rim around it. I sighed as I walked outside and climbed into the boat.

"Are you mad?" He didn't look at me.

"As much as I want to be, I'm not. I don't know why." He looked down at his hand.

"Why won't you look at me?" I looked over at him, starting to get frustrated.

"I just can't, not right now. I told you not to come, and you came. I didn't want you to see my mom like this; I didn't want you to see me like this. I know it's a lot to take in, and my mom can be a big pain in the ass. But now that you have, I'm just afraid that you won't see me the same." He started to rub his burnt hand which was bright red; you could see little blisters forming. I stood up.

"I shouldn't have come, but I had to see you. I'm sorry. I wanted to formally ask you to come to my dad's wedding with me, but I will understand if I just ruined that." I leaned down and kissed his forehead before setting the wedding invitation beside him. I sighed as I looked back at him and walked off.

CHAPTER 13

I woke up to the sound of my alarm blaring telling me it was time to go to school. It had been a week since I talked to Bryan, or Chase. It seemed like Chase had even more girls attached to him lately. Like he knew it bothered me, so he kept doing it. I was angry; no, angry was an understatement. I was furious. I thought I knew Chase better than that. A part of me felt like I was being unfair to Chase, because I didn't know how Bryan would act if we went to the same school. But I doubt it was like what Chase was doing. I knew Bryan better than that. I felt bad that the thought even crossed my mind. I missed Bryan. I didn't have a chance to miss Chase, because I saw him every day. But Bryan, he deserved better. He deserved everything I knew I lacked. Everything I couldn't give him. After I got totally ready for school, my mom came into my room.

"Katie? What are you doing?" I looked at her confused.

"You're not going to school today. You're going up to your fathers to help him prepare for the wedding tomorrow." I groaned, but nodded. I couldn't get in a fight with my mom.

"Is there something you aren't telling me? Did

something happen between you and Chase? I haven't seen him around lately. I miss his smile and come to think of it, I miss your smile, too." I just looked at her. I wanted to tell her my frown had nothing to do with Chase. Well, only partially.

"No, everything is not fine mom. I ruined it. I always do. He's mad at me and I don't know what to do." I knew she thought I was talking about Chase, and I wanted it to be about him. But deep down, I knew I was talking about Bryan. The fact that Chase was mad at me had barely crossed my mind after my fight with Bryan. He was the reason my smile was gone. At least that's what I thought.

My mom sighed. "Katie, if you really want to fix this, I'm sure you can."

I shook my head and stood up. "I'm just going to head to dad's." My mom nodded.

When we were about to leave my room, Mike came out of nowhere and said, "Are you two really talking about boys?"

I shook my head. "No, why would we do that?" I looked back at my mom, who laughed and said, "Of course."

I said, "Bye, guys." I walked downstairs and went out the front door to my car.

When I got in the car to start driving, my mind wandered back to Bryan and Chase. They were totally different and I felt like I needed both of them, but for different reasons. Chase was my best friend who I had accidently fallen in love with. He knew how to make me smile, even on my worst days. But then there was Bryan. He was the sweetest guy I had ever met, and he understands me like no one else does. It's like he gets it. I trust him completely. I knew I couldn't lead both of them on any longer. It just wasn't fair to them anymore.

My mind began to dig deeper into what I really wanted. Suddenly, a thought came to me and I slammed on my brakes. It's lucky nobody ever drove on this dusty road except for the occasional tractors and horses. I leaned my head against the steering wheel as I began to put the pieces together. It hit me hard. I realized I wasn't just choosing between Chase and Bryan. I was choosing between my mom and my dad. That was a choice I couldn't make. I realized that the harder my mom pushed Chase towards me, the more I wanted him. But knowing that Bryan meant spending time with my dad, I always wanted to go back.

I continued driving through my dad's gate. I wasn't sure if I was capable of choosing between my parents. I never had to make that choice before. My mom has always chosen that for me, by not letting me go see my dad. I parked my car outside my dad's house and got out. When I was walking up the porch steps, I heard my dad's voice. I smiled at the sound of it. As I walked in the door, I could hear footsteps walking toward me. My dad engulfed me in a hug. I smiled as I kissed his cheek. He was starting to grow a goatee; I guess he was getting lazy before the wedding. I smiled up at him.

"Katie, Carrie needs to talk to you. Please be open-minded, at least for your old man." I laughed and pushed his shoulder playfully. All of a sudden, Carrie was behind me. She grabbed my arm and jerked me towards the other room. When I turned around, I saw that she was wearing a pink sundress with brown ankle boots. I looked towards her face.

"Look, I know you said you didn't want to be my bridesmaid, but one of my friends who was supposed to replace you is in the hospital. Of all weeks! I mean, if she would have gone into the hospital next week I wouldn't have cared as much. She is so selfish. Does she not know how important this week is for me?" I looked at her in disbelief and cleared my throat.

"And the point is?"

"Right. The point is, I need you to be one of my bridesmaids. It's just, I need—"

"Okay."

"I need five and I'm down to four…wait, it's really okay? Wow, that was easy. Well, your dress is on your bed. I guess that's it." I walked out of the room and looked down at my arm which had a red handprint on it now. That woman had a grip. I ran upstairs to my room and after moving the dress out of the way, fell down on my bed. I didn't want to think about my problems right now. I wanted to escape them, at least for a while. I couldn't handle anymore. I just needed someone to care, anyone.

CHAPTER 14

I woke up to the thought that today was the day my dad was going to alter not only his life, but mine as well. There was a light tapping sound at my door. I sat up in my bed as I said, "Come in." I smiled when I saw my dad walk in, clean shaven and looking happy.

"Hey, kiddo. You're finally up." I nodded as I looked at my clock. It was noon. Guests would start arriving at 4:00. I was happy that my dad had persuaded Carrie to have the ceremony at the house. If we weren't having it here, I would have been up hours ago. I got out of bed and walked over to my big window that overlooked the backyard. As I pulled the blinds back, I gasped. About an acre into our land, where only green grass used to be, there were two sections of white chairs. Between the two sections was a red carpet covered with white rose petals. The flower girls were going to be throwing purple petals. The carpet led to a white gazebo that was surrounded by red and purple flowers. Then closer to the house, where the reception was going to be held, were white tables with red roses in the middle of each. The roses were in clear vases with light brown rocks in the bottom of them. There was a path that led from the reception part to the ceremony part, which was lined with white flowers.

I looked over at my dad. "Wow! That's beautiful. I

didn't picture your big day to be like this."

He laughed and walked up behind me. He put his arm around my shoulder and said, "It's what Carrie wanted."

I looked up at him. "Is it what you want?" Usually he was the one asking me about my life choices. Now it was my turn.

"I want her to be happy. So if this—" and he gestured outside "—makes her happy, then that's what I want."

I looked down at the window seat. "Is this how it was with mom? Is that how you felt?" I could feel his eyes looking down at me and I couldn't look up.

"That's complicated. That was my goal for so long. But as time passed, I wasn't making her happy anymore. It was just time to move on. Now she has Mike and I have Carrie. I guess it worked out for the best. Don't you think?"

I leaned my head against the window. "I guess."

He put his hand on my cheek and made me look at him. "Is there something you aren't telling me?"

"No, dad, of course not. Look, I have to get ready, so——"

He put his hands up. "Got it. I'm gone." He laughed and was about to walk out when he turned around. "I love you, Katie. You'll always be my little girl." He gave me a hug and then walked out of my room, closing the door behind him.

It was nearing four o'clock and I was almost out of time to get ready. My hair was being worn down with loose curls, with my bangs pulled back into a small poof. I smiled at myself in the mirror. After the final touches to my hair, I walked out of the bathroom and put on my peach bridesmaid dress. She had decided to change the color from blue to peach. I guess to prove a point, not that the point was received. I looked at myself in the mirror for the last time and sighed. This was it. I didn't have any more moves up my sleeve to make Carrie see she wasn't welcome in my family. I knew it was time for me to face it and grow up. I was beginning to realize that life was unpredictable. If Lucas' death taught me anything, it was that nothing is guaranteed. Life can be over in a second. So if I had to be happy in front of my dad, I would; because I could lose him, and I wouldn't want his last memory of me to be a bad one. I would do it, for him.

I walked into the next room where the other bridesmaids and the soon-to-be-bride were gathered and I froze.

"Carrie, you're actually...you look beautiful." She just stared at me and followed my compliment with a sarcastic remark.

I sighed and went to sit on the couch in the corner of the room realizing it was no use being nice to her. If I wasn't putting on a brave face for my dad, I would have had a comment back to her. I was gazing out the window when someone opened the door and walked in. I looked over to see the wedding planner, Missy, looking at me.

"Katie, someone is downstairs looking for you." I nodded and got up. She let me walk past her. When I was downstairs, I looked out the back window and saw a lot of guests taking their seats. I walked to the front of the house where my mom was and hugged her.

"Hey, mom, were you looking for me?"

She looked at me. "Hey, baby. No, I wasn't. I'm waiting for Mike." I looked back toward the house where Missy was calling my name.

"Katie, someone is looking for you in the back!" I looked at my mom and smiled.

"See you later."

I walked to the back of the house where the reception was going to be taking place. In the middle of the dance floor, he was standing there, with a single rose in one of his hands. I ran over to him.

"Bryan!" I kissed him lightly. I was happy he was here. He was wearing a black suit with a light blue button down shirt, with a black and light blue patterned tie. "I didn't think you were going to come." He smiled down at me and handed me the rose.

"Oh, come on Katie, I promised I would be here. Besides, my word is the most important thing to me. You need me here anyway so you won't look too bad when you're dancing." I laughed and pushed against his chest playfully. He studied me carefully for a second. "How are you doing with all of this?"

I sighed as I grabbed one of his hands. I could feel my eyes watering up. "I don't want him to marry her.

There is something telling me he shouldn't, but what am I supposed to do? I'm not going to tell him. I just…I certainly don't want him to be alone anymore."

He pulled me against his chest and kissed the top of my head. "It's okay. Everything is going to work out. I promise." I looked up at him and smiled as I wiped my eyes.

"Well, you better go and I better get back there and find a seat. Oh, by the way, you look beautiful." He smiled and kissed my nose lightly, then turned to walk away. I looked down at the rose and smiled. When he was a few feet away he turned around and said, "And I almost forgot…that rose came from the back table." He chuckled as he continued walking to his seat.

I looked to the back row of tables and saw that one of the tables was missing a rose in the vase. I chuckled to myself as I quickly walked over to the table and returned the rose. When I walked inside, everyone was lining up with the person they were going to walk with. I was going to be walking with Gary, one of my dad's oldest friends. Gary was practically family. I smiled as I walked over to him.

At this point, we were supposed to be quiet and get ready, so I silently slid my arm into his. When the music started playing, the flower girls were the first to walk down the aisle as they threw the purple rose petals on the ground. When they got to the front we all slowly walked down the aisle in line. I took my place between two of the other bridesmaids, Susie and

Veronica. When the last of the bridesmaids were down the aisle, the wedding march started to play and Carrie started to walk down the aisle with her father. I looked over at my dad who was smiling. I could see his eyes filling with emotion. At this moment, I was actually happy that he was happy; as much as it hurt me, his happiness outweighed anything I was feeling.

When the ceremony started, I couldn't take my eyes off my dad. He looked different. It might have just been that his hair was actually fixed instead of him just pushing it down with water and his hands. I wasn't sure. They were almost to the vows part and I wanted to scream, "Don't marry her!" But I couldn't find my voice. I looked down at my feet when the preacher asked if anyone had any objections. I wanted to raise my hand, but I couldn't. Out of nowhere, I heard a familiar voice.

"You can't marry her." I looked up and saw Bryan standing up, looking at me. I smiled slightly at what he was doing.

I looked over at my dad as he said, "Bryan, what are you doing?"

Bryan looked over at him, "I'm sorry, sir. But I can't let you marry her."

My dad looked angry. "What are you talking about?" My dad looked at the preacher and said, "He's just a kid, he doesn't know what he's talking about."

Suddenly the preacher said, "Young man, do you

have a reason why these two people shouldn't get married?" Bryan glanced over at me then back at the preacher.

"Yes, sir." He looked over at my dad again. "Sir, have you ever asked Katie what she felt about this? This is affecting her, just as much as it is affecting your whole family. This one event can change her life. Doesn't she have any say in that?"

My dad looked over at me then back at Bryan. "I asked her. She would have said something." He looked over at me. "Kat, you would have told me, right?" I looked over at him and could feel my eyes fill with tears, because I knew the truth; and I knew how much it would hurt him. I shook my head.

"I'm sorry, dad. I can't-" I looked down at my shoes, then looked back at my dad when he let go of Carrie's hands.

Suddenly Carrie shouted, "Whoa, I don't know what's happening here, but I don't like it." She looked over at my dad. "You can't believe Katie." My dad took a staggered step back.

"I'm really sorry, Carrie, but my daughter means too much to me to not listen to her."

I smiled at my dad as he walked over to me and hugged me.

Carried screamed, "You're going to regret this." She walked down from the gazebo and into the house.

My dad smiled then turned to the guests. "Well, we have all this food, and a DJ. Everyone is welcome to stay and have a good time." Some of the guests from the bride's side got up and left, but everyone from my dad's side walked over to the reception area. I looked up at my dad.

"Thanks, Dad. I love you." He smiled down at me.

"We'll talk about this later, kiddo. Right now, I want to dance with my daughter."

I smiled as he walked me over to the dance floor where other people were already dancing. Suddenly, a slow song came on and my dad pulled me to him and started to dance. I laughed.

"How can you be in a good mood after what just happened?"

"Let's just say I've had a lot of practice putting on a mask. It hurts a little, Katie, but sometimes you see things I don't. I love you, kid. I guess it's back to you and me." He smiled. We danced for about half of the song when Bryan walked up.

"May I cut in?" I smiled over at him, but was scared at what my dad was going to say.

My dad looked calm and replied, "You sure can. I'm starving anyway. Oh, thanks for sticking up for Katie earlier. It's really appreciated. She needs someone to look after her." He smiled and walked away. Bryan put his arms around my waist as I put my arms on his shoulders.

I looked up at him, "Thank you. I owe you a lot."

He smiled, "You don't owe me. You just being here with me is enough. Listen, I'm sorry for how I acted when you showed up at my house. That was…wrong."

I sighed and said, "You don't need to be apologizing, if anyone needs to, it's me. You told me not to come to your house. I should have respected that." I stretched up to kiss him. When I pulled away, I leaned my head against his chest. We kept dancing into the next song. About halfway through the song, someone pulled me away from Bryan until his arms were straight and I had to stretch to reach his shoulders.

"Please keep arm's length away." I looked over at Mike, who had a big smile on his face and surprisingly, no baseball hat. I laughed and hugged him.

"Mike, this is Bryan. Bryan, this is my step dad, Mike." They shook hands. "Where's Mom?"

Mike smiled. "She brought something for you. She went to get it." I nodded. It was kind of awkward having Mike meet my boyfriend before my mom did. When my mom walked back over, she didn't have anything with her. She came over and hugged me. She looked at Bryan.

"Katie, who's this?"

I smiled. "Bryan, this is my mom. Mom, this is Bryan, my boyfriend."

My mom inhaled deeply. "Boyfriend?"

I put my hand lightly on my mom's shoulder. "Mom, are you okay?" When I touched her, it looked like it brought her out of whatever trance she was in.

She stretched out her hand. "It's nice to meet you, Bryan. I'm glad she hasn't been hanging out alone, with all the time she has been spending down here lately because of the wedding and all."

I smiled, "Well, Bryan and I are going to go dance." I turned and let Bryan lead me away from my parents. I could see my mom still staring at us and I didn't know why. I rested my hands on Bryan's chest as he wrapped his arms around my waist, then leaned down to kiss me. It was a deep kiss that was rudely interrupted by a familiar voice.

"Katie?" I looked over and saw Chase.

"Chase? What are you doing here?" I looked up at Bryan, who looked confused.

"Your mom told me you wanted me to be your date."

Chase looked over at Bryan. "But I can see you have that covered." His eyes flickered back to me. "Were you playing both of us?"

Bryan let go of his grip around my waist and put his hands in his pockets. "Katie, what is he talking about?"

Chase looked over at Bryan. "Don't pretend you don't already know."

"Alright, let's calm down. Let her explain." Bryan rested his hand on Chase's shoulder to calm him down.

Chase looked down at Bryan's hand. "Big mistake." Before I knew what he was doing, Chase punched Bryan in the eye. When Bryan recovered, he punched Chase in the side of the head, then kicked him in the groin and Chase fell to the ground. When Chase got his bearings, he grabbed a chair that was the closest to him and slammed it into the back of Bryan's legs. The impact made Bryan fall to his knees.

I yelled, "Chase, stop!" He looked at me in disbelief, then shook his head, stood up, and walked off.

"Chase!" I ran after him, grabbed his hand and turned him around. "Wait!"

He looked at me and said, "Let me get this straight, Katie. You told me you weren't ready, so you left me there waiting for you to finally be ready." He was getting more angry and his eyes were turning red like he was trying to hold back tears. "I was here the whole time. But then you come here and all of a sudden, you're ready. When you left for your dad's and came back, I could tell you were different. All of a sudden, I wasn't good enough."

He turned to walk away, but turned around with one last parting remark. "It's a good thing Lucas died, because you would have done the exact same thing to him; except you would have been playing three guys."

I stood there in shock for a couple of minutes. When I finally stopped tearing up, I walked back to find Bryan. I finally found him sitting in one of the chairs where the botched ceremony was held. I walked up behind him, but stopped when he started talking.

"He was supposed to be your date. Please tell me you weren't dating him, too."

I shook my head, "No, I'm only dating you." Bryan stood up and faced me, and I saw that he was starting to cry.

"Then why did your mom bring him? Why did he say that you were playing him?"

I shook my head, "I don't know why she brought him, but I wouldn't say I was playing him."

Bryan looked down at his shoes. "Then what would you say?"

My nose started to sting like it did before I started crying. I was at a loss for words. I shook my head lightly. Bryan looked up at me after a few seconds when I didn't say anything. He stood up and took a step closer to me so that we were face-to-face. He looked me in the eyes as he asked, "Do you love him?"

"I…I wouldn't say that." At that moment, my eyes overflowed and a single tear rolled down my face, followed by more.

"How would you say it?"

"I didn't mean to love him."

Bryan looked up at the sky defeated. "I can't believe this. I don't even know who you are anymore." He started to walk away.

"Don't walk away! That's not what happened! You don't understand." He turned and walked up to me. We were so close I could feel his breath on my face when he spoke.

"Then explain it to me. Because you're right, I don't get it." I just stood there and he breathed out heavily. "You can't even explain it, because all he said and everything I said are true. I trusted you. Out of all the crap that has been going on in my life, you were the one good thing. The one thing I could look forward to. But now, I don't even have that." He turned and walked away.

"Bryan! Don't walk away!" I fell to my knees. With everything that just happened, all I could think about was what Bryan's mom said when she was sitting there weak and fragile telling me not to break Bryan's heart. I couldn't move. I not only broke his heart, but mine as well.

CHAPTER 15

I didn't want to wake up because I knew what happened the day before wasn't a dream. I knew my heart wasn't in one piece anymore. I knew I ruined my dad's wedding. I wanted it to be a dream. I wanted the comfort of Bryan and Chase for when I visited both of my parents. Now I didn't have that and I was scared.

I walked downstairs after I got my head together and found my dad cooking pancakes. My dad? Cooking? I was suddenly not hungry. I just stood there watching him set the table and put the big stack of pancakes next to the pitcher of orange juice. As I walked to the table, I noticed the vineyard was starting to grow, it was huge now. My dad saw where I was looking.

"It's getting pretty big. I might hire workers for the summer." He smiled at me as I walked to the table and sat down.

I said, "That might be a good idea, because me out in the sun all day isn't the best thing." I laughed.

"Oh, good. So that means you're still going to visit your old man in the summer." He smiled over at me as I nodded. I took a big bite out of one of the pancakes and surprisingly, it wasn't that bad. I could feel my dad's eyes on me, studying me. I looked up at him from the corner of my eye.

"What?"

"I'm trying to figure out why you didn't tell me how you felt about Carrie."

I just shrugged, "I couldn't do that to you. You were so happy. I couldn't take that away from you. Plus, I live with mom most of the time and if I took Carrie away from you, then you would be all alone." I looked up at my dad who looked like he was deep in thought, so I had to break the silence. "Please say something."

My dad just shrugged. "I don't know what to say. I can't believe that you were sacrificing how you felt for me to be happy. Isn't that something a dad is supposed to do, not the daughter?" He glanced at me and all I could do was smile. "Is anything wrong? For example, what happened with Bryan and that other boy? It looked intense and I'm not just saying that because they got in a brawl."

I shook my head. "It wasn't like that. Well, yes it was. I don't even know what happened. Back home I met Chase and we had a connection, but I wasn't over Lucas. Then I come here and there was something different with Bryan; but it doesn't even matter now because they found out and left."

I looked up at my dad when he asked, "What do you want?"

"I want everything to be right. I want someone to just show me a path and say this is the guy you should choose. What do I do?"

My dad sighed. "I think they both deserve an

apology. Go see Bryan, then talk to Chase tomorrow at school." I groaned. "Or if you don't want to do that, you could just give up on boys until you're 30."

I chuckled. "Yeah, right. Did stuff like this ever happen to you when you were my age?"

My dad laughed, "Are you kidding? Not to me because I was a ladies' man. You have two arms for a reason." I looked down at my plate. "Okay, that was a bad joke and bad timing, too." He gently laid his hand on mine. "I know you'll do what's right, Katie, you always do." He kissed the top of my head before he started to walk towards the back door.

As he placed his hand on the doorknob, I asked, "Hey, dad?"

He glanced at me, "Yeah?"

"We're going to be alright, right?" I asked, as my eyebrows pushed together.

My dad looked out the back window before looking back at me with a genuine smile.

"I think we are."

Later that morning, I drove down the familiar driveway leading to the small house that I loved. I was scared, not because I would have to face Bryan; but because I didn't know if I could look Bryan's mom in the face without thinking about the broken promise. When I parked my car and got out, I heard a crash from the garage on the side of the house. I ran over to see Bryan bent over a faded red truck. He was doing something with the engine. He was wearing brown cargo shorts with a white tank top and draped over one shoulder, he had a blue short-sleeve button down shirt. When I looked down, I saw he was wearing blue Jordan's. I smiled.

"Bryan?" He looked back at me. He had grease all over his hands and some of it going up his arm. He also had some mixed in his hair and on his face.

"Why are you here?" Before I could answer, he turned around and started messing with something.

"I came to say I'm sorry. What I did was stupid. I'm just really confused and didn't know what to do. Are you listening?"

He didn't turn around, but he shouted at me. "Sorry, can't hear over all the lies."

I walked over to him and grabbed his shoulder and turned him around.

"Stop treating me like this! Is this what you're really like? When someone makes a mistake, you just ignore them and act like a spoiled brat? Really, Bryan?"

Bryan rolled his eyes. "Oh, please, do you know what you're talking about? Me spoiled, really? Do you even know what it's like to have to work for something? I pay all the bills, the electricity, the water, the house insurance, the car insurance, and all of the medical bills. I work pretty much every day, while balancing school work. Then in my free time, I get to take care of my drunken mom. So excuse me if I don't have a little sympathy for you. Do you want to tell me how I should treat you? Last time I checked, I got hurt. You said it yourself...you're confused, which means you're not. Don't try turning this on me. I tried to give you everything I had, and the one thing I wanted was for you to do the same. Just go."

I shook my head. "Isn't it my choice where I belong?"

He nodded, "Yes, but since you're confused, I'm making it easier on you. I'm not going to make you choose."

"What are you fixing anyway? Is this how you cope with the pain, by getting all greasy and sweaty?"

He chuckled sarcastically. "Excuse me? It's my dad's truck, the one that ran into the lake. I've wanted to fix it for a long time, but up until recently I wanted to be with you as much as I could. Now I have a lot of extra time on my hands since we aren't together. I'm serious, Katie. Leave."

"We're over?"

Bryan looked at me confused. "Did you really not know that? You cheated on me. We aren't going to stay together. That's not how it works. I know that might be a new concept for you."

"Bryan, I—"

He put his hand up, "Katie! Really, I don't want to hear it. Please just go. You don't belong here." I couldn't say anything after that, so I just turned and walked away. The last memory I was going to have of Bryan was him covered in grease and in pain. As I walked to my car with a failed apology, I hoped my next apology wasn't going to be a failure as well. Next up, Chase.

CHAPTER 16

My heart started to thump louder than it ever has before. I could almost feel it in every part of my body. How did people do this? How do they face every problem in their life head on? I could barely face two guys, two guys that I loved, two guys that loved me.

As I pulled into Chase's driveway, I tried to calm myself down. After a couple of deep breaths, I climbed out of my car and walked slowly to the door. It seemed like it took forever for me to get there. When I finally stepped onto his porch, I took one more deep breath and knocked on the door. I knew he was home because his garage door was open revealing his Hummer; and I also knew his mom wasn't, because she worked Sundays. I was about to turn around when Chase opened the door. His facial expression went from a smile to a frown quicker than you can snap your fingers. He was wearing a plain red shirt with blue jeans and his white vans. I was suddenly afraid of what his reaction would be to me at his door after I had "played him," to use his words. He shoved one of his hands in a pocket as he kept the other one on the door. He took a deep breath as he looked at the floor. After it was clear that he wasn't going to say the first word, I broke the silence.

"Can we talk?"

He sighed and leaned against the door frame. "I have nothing to say to you."

"Chase, seriously? You're acting like a first grader. Grow up."

"Are you kidding me, Katie? What, now I'm not mature enough for you?"

I sighed and looked down at the ground, but then out of nowhere a wave of strength came through me. "If you're not going to invite me in, then I'll let myself in." I pushed against his chest and slid around him. He looked at me in shock. "You said I was welcome anytime." That broke him and a big smile came across his face, which he quickly tried to hide.

"That was before everything happened."

"Nothing has changed, Chase. You were and still are my best friend. I'm not going to lose you over something that stupid." He leaned his head on the back of the door frame.

"No, being your best friend isn't good enough anymore. I can't go back to just being your best friend, your confidant. I can't. I tried, I did, and I gave it my all. But I can't." He shrugged and closed his eyes for a second.

All I could do was look down at the floor. "You're making me choose?"

"You kind of have to, because you can't have both of us."

I shook my head. "I can't make that choice right now. I'm not sure about anything anymore. What makes you think I can handle choosing something that is going to change my life forever?"

I heard him walk over to me, but didn't realize how close he was until he pulled me to his chest. It felt good to be back in his arms, but something was pulling at my heartstrings. I suddenly felt guilty because they weren't the arms I wanted around me, but I wasn't sure which ones I needed around me.

He sighed and said, "I think you already made your choice."

I looked up at him. "What are you talking about?"

He laughed. "Aren't you supposed to be the smart one? You're here. If you wanted him, you'd be over there. Plus, your home is here. It's the only place you belong."

I could only nod. I thought that my voice would break if I tried to speak. Chase gently slid his hand under my chin and started to lean down to kiss me, though he was giving me time to pull away. But right now, I didn't have the strength or the will to push away. The kiss was different than the last one. The last kiss was more of a force, it was hard. But this one was warm and slow. I smiled as he pulled away. I laid my head against his chest as he kissed the top of my head. "Welcome home." I smiled at that thought. Home. But something didn't feel right, something was missing. Could I really just leave everything that happened at my dad's house? Could it really be that easy just to forget about it and move on? I knew that's what I did with

Lucas, but I didn't have a choice with him. Lucas was just gone, I didn't choose for him to leave.

When I woke up the next morning, I realized it was going to be the first day Chase and I walked into school hand-in-hand. Everyone would know, but nobody would be surprised. They all knew it was going to happen, except me. I walked over to my closet and took out my favorite pair of jeans, a black tank top with my black and white striped cardigan. I looked in the mirror after I straightened my hair and smiled. I heard a honk outside of my house and smiled as I saw Chase, my boyfriend, waiting in his Hummer. I started to second guess my choice, but I realized that I made the right one. Chase had been right; my life was here, my mom was here, and I had to be with her. At the beginning, Chase was there to bring me back. Bryan just gave me the push I needed to get back out there. What Bryan did counted a lot, but without Chase, Bryan wouldn't have had anything to boost up. I walked downstairs and met Chase at the door. As soon as I opened the door, I noticed the bright smile on his face. How could he go so fast from being pissed one day to being happy the next day? Sometimes I just didn't understand him. I laughed as he pulled me into a hug.

When we got in the car, I looked over at him and caught him looking back at me. I laughed and punched him lightly on the shoulder. "What?"

"If I knew you were going to look like this, I would have made you choose sooner."

I laughed. "Shut up. Don't start expecting this. You're lucky I was in a good mood this morning."

He smiled. "Oh, you know I'm going to be expecting this." I smiled and watched as Chase pulled into the school parking lot. So far, nothing was different. He always drove me to school and he always drove me home. When he parked his Hummer in its regular place, I took a deep breath. This was it. I hoped this is what I wanted, what I needed. But now that I look back, Chase had always been there, through everything, so it felt right with him. But I couldn't help but feel as if something was missing. It felt wrong to feel this way. This wasn't how it was supposed to be. I wasn't supposed to be feeling any doubt, right? I didn't know anymore. I don't know how long I just sat there staring out the window. It couldn't have been more than a few minutes. But Chase didn't complain, he just sat waiting patiently. After a while, he lightly grabbed my hand. I snapped out of whatever trance I was in and looked over at him.

"Everything good?"

I just nodded. I didn't know if I could talk. He chuckled and said, "Okay, well, we don't want to be late for class."

I nodded and stepped out of the car. As we walked through school holding hands, I realized there was no going back now, no running for cover and no hiding anything. Now that our secret was out, everyone would know. Everyone.

CHAPTER 17

It felt like my junior year had flown by. I couldn't believe it was summer, the summer before my senior year to be exact. This was the last year of high school for me. It was the one that was supposed to be carefree; the one that everyone was going to remember for the rest of their lives. It was the one that counted.

It was the first day of summer and I was bored. Chase had flown to Atlanta to visit his grandparents and unfortunately, he didn't have a set date when he was coming back. He was staying at least a week, but I had a feeling it was going to be longer than that. I remembered the night before he left. He had taken me to one of the nicest restaurants in town. He had said it was a celebration for the school year ending.

After the waiter had taken our order, I looked over at Chase and smiled. He looked like he was nervous about something, so I reached across the table and took his hand.

"Are you okay?" I asked.

He nodded, "I have something for you. He slid his hand into his pocket and pulled out a box. He handed the box to me and when I opened it, I gasped. Inside there was a necklace, it was silver and had a heart dangling from the chain.

"Chase, it's…beautiful." I couldn't help but stutter the words, because I thought beautiful was an understatement. At the same time, saying a necklace was gorgeous sounded weird to me. I looked up at him and he had a bright smile on his face.

"Here, let me help you put it on." He got up from his seat and walked around the table to me. He gently took the necklace from my hand and put it around my neck. When he was done, he leaned down and kissed my cheek. "Happy three-month anniversary."

I froze. Three months. Had it really been that long? I hadn't seen my dad in three months! That made me feel horrible, because I messed up his wedding and then left him alone for three months. I knew he had gotten help for the vineyard, so he had those people. But they were working, too busy to socialize with him. He reached his seat and sat back down. "So when I go to Atlanta, what are you going to do without me?" He chuckled because I knew he meant it as a joke, but I took it seriously.

"I actually think I might go see my dad." The smile vanished from his lips. I knew what he was thinking… Bryan. He was still a little tense about the whole thing, but he was usually better at hiding it.

"Chase, it's my dad."

"I know. But *he's* there."

"I'm dating you!"

"But you dated him. Look, I know you still care about him. I know you still probably love him."

I shook my head. "That's not true."

"Katie, that's b.s. You can't lie to me. I'm not saying you don't love me; I'm just saying that maybe"…he held up his hands…"you love both of us."

"I haven't even seen him in three months. I—"

"Exactly, but when you do see him, your feelings might come rushing back. I can't lose you, but I also don't want to wait around for you to be okay with only one of us." That was the end of the conversation. I wasn't going to talk to him about this anymore and I made that very clear when I stood up and walked out of the restaurant. By the time I made it outside the glass doors, Chase had already caught up to me. "Katie, wait up. I'm sorry."

I stopped and swung around. "Do you really not trust me?"

He shook his head, "No, of course I do. It's just hard. You chose him over me once and you could do it again."

"But I wasn't dating you then, I'm dating you now." I walked up to him and put my hands on both sides of his face. "You have nothing to worry about." I leaned up to kiss him. When I pulled away, Chase cleared his throat and asked, "Are you ready to go back inside now?" I nodded and let him lead the way.

As I thought back to that night, I started to think that maybe he was right; maybe I did love both of them. But these past few months, the feelings that I had for Bryan had been in the shadows. They had been hiding. As I was driving to my dad's, that simple truth hit me. I knew what I had to do while I was here. I had to avoid him, I couldn't risk it. My relationship with Chase was going too well for me to ruin it. I couldn't do that to Chase. I knew it was going to be difficult to ignore Bryan, but I had to do it. I would just have to stay away from the barn and resist the urge to drive to his house.

I signed as I pulled into my dad's driveway. I hadn't told him I was coming; I decided that I would surprise him. I got my bag out of the back seat and slung it over my back. When I got inside the house, I yelled, "Hello? Dad?"

I saw the back of his head on the patio that over-looked the vineyard in the backyard. I walked upstairs and set my stuff down on the bed. After I touched up my hair, I went outside. My mouth dropped when I saw the vineyard; it was huge. It had to be twice the size it was three months ago. I was still staring when my dad turned around.

"Katie?" He stood up with a big smile on his face and walked towards me. "What are you doing here?"

I smiled and hugged him. "I missed you, so I thought I would drop in for a visit. How have you been, Dad?"

He nodded. "Good, a little lonely without you,

but…" I pushed him lightly and he laughed. "Nah, I've been good. I hired enough workers to help me with the vineyard and they're a crazy bunch of guys." He looked out to the vineyard and said, "Let me show it to you." He smiled. I couldn't say no to that.

As we started walking, he said, "So since you haven't been here in awhile, I'm guessing you and Bryan are done for good?"

I sighed. "Dad, we tried, it didn't work out."

"You don't seem too bummed about it."

I shook my head. "I can't talk about this. I have a boyfriend and he's a good guy, really."

"Whoa, kiddo, why are you so defensive? I didn't say he wasn't. It seems to me like you're trying to convince yourself to like this guy."

"No, of course not."

My dad just nodded and looked at me, his wise eyes filled with knowledge. "Good, you can't force love, Katie. It just happens." I nodded. As we rounded the corner to go onto another row of the vineyard, I ran into someone. I saw cowboy boots and jeans over the boots. My eyes went up a little further and I saw a grey and brown flannel shirt, sleeves rolled up to the elbows. I also saw a familiar leather necklace with a cross dangling from it and a brown cowboy hat.

All I could say was, "Oh, I'm so sorry. I wasn't watching where I was going." I looked up at his face and immediately backed up. "Bryan?"

I heard my dad clear his throat. "Was that the phone? I think it's ringing. I'm just going to go see who that is." He walked away and I watched him with my eyes narrowed; he would do that. I looked up at Bryan and saw he was carrying a big pair of pliers.

"I'm sorry. I should have been watching where I was going." He turned his back to me and started trimming the leaves around the berries. I was about to walk away when my mouth decided it had other plans.

Out of nowhere, I said, "How have you been?"

He chuckled and it was not a happy chuckle. It sounded mean.

"What are you doing, Katie?" His reaction set something off in me and suddenly, I couldn't show weakness.

"I was just asking how you're doing."

"Why would you do that? You left three months ago without so much as a phone call, and you expect me to believe that all of a sudden you care again? Katie, just because I live in the country and dropped out of school doesn't make me stupid."

"You dropped out of school?"

"Why do you think I got a job here full time? I get two days a week off, and during those two days I work at the barn."

"Why do you need two jobs?"

"My mom is completely incapable of having a job at the moment and we were about to lose our house. I pay all the bills, I pay for my gas, I pay for the groceries, and I pay for the beer." He shook his head, "I don't even know why I'm telling you this."

"Bryan, I—"

"Katie! That's enough. I have to finish my work. I have plans tonight."

"You're going on a date?"

"I still don't get why it matters to you. We—" and pointed between us— "don't have anything, not anymore. You're not the only one that is allowed to see someone else."

I looked at him shocked. I didn't think he knew about Chase. "Yeah, I know about Chase. It's a small town, remember? News gets around." He turned to walk away, but I grabbed his hand and stopped him.

"I just want to be friends, Bryan."

He jerked his hand away. "It's too late for that Katie, I'm sorry. I-I can't." He started to walk away again and I let him. I sighed and walked back up to the house. When I got up to the patio, there were two men sitting on the steps. When they saw me approach, they stood up and one of them said, "You must be Katie, the boss' daughter, right? I've heard a lot about you." He reached his hand toward me and I shook it. "I'm Scotty Barnes."

I smiled. "Nice to meet you."

Scotty was wearing jeans with a plain white shirt and a black cowboy hat. I could see some of his blonde hair sticking out under the sides of his hat. He had blue eyes.

The man next to Scotty cleared his throat and stood up. "I'm Sam Barnes." He also extended his hand for me to shake.

I smiled as I grabbed his hand. "So are y'all brothers?" Sam opened his mouth to answer, but Scotty blurted out, "Twins."

I nodded. Sam looked similar to Scotty except he had brown hair and was wearing a plain red shirt with a brown cowboy hat. They were silent for a few seconds before Scotty said, "So the way your dad talked about the bond you two have, I figured that you'd be up here a lot more."

"I've been really busy with school and all of that."

Sam chuckled. "So it has nothing to do with Bryan and your little drama." I looked at him clueless for a second. "When you work every day with the same guys, you tend to spill secrets and mess around with each other." Both of the guys started laughing.

I smiled. "Well, I guess that was part of the reason at first; but after a while, I just got really swamped with everything. Ya' know what? I better get inside."

Scotty and Sam nodded as Scotty said, "See you tomorrow, and the day after that and the day after that…"

Sam cut Scotty off by pushing him lightly and saying, "She gets it." They both burst out laughing, almost as if it was on cue. I was about to turn and walk inside the house, when I saw a golf cart come around the side of the house. Inside it was a guy that looked a few years older than me and next to him was Bryan. They were both smiling about something, but Bryan's smile faded when he saw me. The guy beside him didn't seem fazed. When the guy saw the twins, he started yelling.

"There you two are. Come on, boys. The back ten have so many weeds, the berries are suffocating!" I looked over at the twins as they took their gardening gloves out of their back pockets and slid them on. They stood up and as they did, Scotty yelled, "Hey! Come meet Charlie's daughter!"

Right after Scotty said that, the golf cart veered off and the man started walking toward me, ignoring the fact that Bryan was yelling, "Come on guys, let's get to work! You can introduce yourselves later!"

I scoffed in his direction, but turned my attention quickly to the man that was now right in front of me.

He extended his hand as he said, "Well, hey there, 'lil lady. My name is Greg and I'm probably the most serious one of this rowdy bunch." He grinned.

I laughed as I responded, "It's nice to meet you. I'm Katie." I let go of his hand when I was distracted by Sam calling out to Bryan.

"Why don't you come join the party?" I looked over at Bryan just in time to see him glance over at me. He shook his head as he said, "Nah, I'm good right here." And to add emphasis to his statement, he put his feet up on the dashboard. Before I knew it, the twins were on the ground walking toward the golf cart. It was like they just jumped off of the porch in a single bound.

They started talking to Bryan, but from the looks of it, it was almost as if they were taunting him. Before long, all three of them were fake fighting before hitting the ground and wrestling. I smiled as I saw that Bryan finally had a smile on his face that lasted a few seconds.

Greg scoffed and said, "Yeah, and I'm the delinquent." He shook his head as he went over to stop the fight, but instead just got sucked up into it. All four of the boys were laughing and throwing fake punches all over the place. About that time, a high pitched whistle came out of nowhere, and all of them straightened up and looked at me. I blushed slightly because I didn't know why they were looking at me. A few milliseconds later, I figured it out when my dad stepped up beside me.

"Gentlemen! Come on! You know I'm all for having fun, but we have about forty minutes of daylight left, alright? And I know y'all work fast, but ten acres in forty minutes is a lot. I know it's been a crazy day with Frankie gone, but let's go, boys. Here." Then my dad threw out a football and Bryan quickly caught it. "From now on, use the football to have fun. Throw it around, play some tackle football." My dad chuckled as all four of the guys started thanking him. "Alright, get to work." Then just like that, all four of them piled into the golf cart and rode off to the back ten acres.

Later that night, my dad decided to take me out for Italian food. As we were walking down the street of the small town, I looked into a Mexican food restaurant and saw Bryan. I looked to see who he was with. I gasped at who I saw him with…Rachel, the girl from the horse stables. I might have been happy for him if it wasn't her.

My dad followed my gaze and laughed. "You don't like seeing Bryan with other girls?"

I rolled my eyes. "I don't care if he's with other girls. I just don't like him with her. He would look better with—"

"You?"

I looked at my dad. "I wasn't going to say that."

My dad nodded. "Yes, you were. You can't lie to me. Just promise me something, okay?"

I nodded. "Anything."

My dad sighed. "Cut Bryan some slack. He's a hard worker, but he's dealing with personal stuff, too. I mean he told me he's thinking of sending his mom to Texas for rehab. He's got a lot of responsibility that he isn't supposed to have."

"Texas? That's far away from here." I started to think about how far New York was from Texas. Would Bryan move with his mom? How could he even think about moving her? I nodded and said, "I promise." My dad then held the front door open for me to Pierre's Italian Restaurant. It felt good being back with my dad. When we were seated at a table, my dad looked over at me and asked, "So what did you think about the guys today?"

I laughed. "Yeah, they are…interesting."

"They're all good guys, especially when everyone has a lot of stress about meeting deadlines. The twins make everyone loosen up. Greg actually started working here as community service, but found a passion for it, so now he works full time and I pretty much have to force him to take vacation time." My dad chuckled and shook his head. "Tomorrow you'll meet Frankie."

"Is he twins with Greg?" I teased.

"Oh, no. We only have room for one set of twins. Frankie is a little younger than me, and was a manager at a vineyard in Tennessee."

I nodded. "Well, I can't wait to meet him. How many acres do we have now anyway?"

My dad smiled. "Well, with the land I bought today, we have roughly 30 acres. That's why they had to weed the land out so late tonight. New land is more work."

CHAPTER 18

The sound of voices woke me up. I walked over to the window and looked out into the backyard. I saw the twins and Greg already moving around in the vineyard. Why were they out so early? Actually, it wasn't that early. I glanced over at my clock and saw it was noon. I put on some denim shorts and a tank top and grabbed my shoulder bag, not sure if I was going to be leaving or not. I walked downstairs and heard my dad talking to someone. As I rounded the corner to go into the kitchen, I saw my dad sitting at the table with, of course, Bryan. They stopped talking when I walked into the room. I smiled as my dad gave me a warm greeting. I looked over at Bryan who looked like he was about to say something to me. But before he got the chance, I walked out of the house and started walking to my car. The ignoring starts now.

When I was about to open my car door, a man nearly my dad's age drove the gator out of the garage with the lawn mower on it. The gator was what my dad used to move large equipment around the vineyard. When the man saw me, he immediately stopped the gator and ran over to me.

"Hey Katie, I'm Frankie. All the boys told me about you and said that they met you yesterday. Sorry I'm a day late, but better late than never."

I smiled as I said, "No, it's fine. You deserved a day off. My dad tells me how hard all of you have been working. I'll let you get back to it. It was nice meeting you." And with that, I climbed into my car and left the property. I had no idea where I was going, but I ended up at the Italian restaurant my dad took me to the night before. I sighed and turned the car around. I didn't know the point of me leaving the house. Without having Bryan with me, I had nowhere to go. I didn't know anyone else. Then I got an idea. If I couldn't have Bryan, that didn't mean I couldn't look out for him. I drove to the barn where he works. When I drove onto the familiar pavement, I sighed. This one area had so many memories. I walked inside and was actually happy when I saw Rachel behind the desk. She looked up when I walked in.

"Good Morning, Rachel."

She just looked at me. "Um…Can I help you?"

I plastered a fake smile to my face. "I came as a friend to Bryan—"

"Friend implies you still talk to him; an ex-girlfriend is something totally different."

I wasn't going to get in a fight with her, I refused to. It would be too easy to reach across the desk and pull out her all too straight dirty blonde hair.

I sighed. "Please, just let me talk. I still care about Bryan. He's a good guy; he deserves the best. Just treat him right."

"Oh, you mean the opposite of how you treated him. Don't worry, I don't have another guy. Unlike you, he has my whole attention. Why do you care anyway?"

I was close to jumping over the desk and plucking out her hair strand by strand, so I decided to get out of there before things got ugly. I turned around and went home. When I got there, I saw Bryan walking toward me and I quickly turned the other way. I saw his reflection through the window and saw that when I turned, he threw his hands up in the air then put them behind his head. I looked down at my shoes while I walked, fighting the urge to run back to him.

The next day, I realized I had successfully avoided Bryan for two days no matter how much it hurt me. I didn't know if I was strong enough to last three days, but I was going to try. I trudged downstairs slowly. When I made it to the bottom of the stairs, I decided to take a walk, so I went out through the garage. When I was halfway down the driveway, a familiar truck rolled up. It was Bryan. He wasn't supposed to be working today. A smile came to my face which I had to quickly hide. He stopped his truck abruptly and jumped out. He was wearing pink vans and white cargo shorts, with a pink shirt with two big horizontal white stripes on it.

He walked up to me and asked, "Are you done ignoring me?"

I chuckled sarcastically. "What? Me? No...Avoiding and ignoring are two completely different things."

Bryan just stared at me with a blank expression on his face like he was waiting for a real answer. I was intending to be silent until he said something, but after a few minutes I broke and said, "Rachel? Really, Bryan!"

"What are you talking about?"

"Your new girlfriend; you can do better than Rachel." He looked down at the ground, then back up at me.

"Why does it matter to you? You have Chase."

"Look, Bryan, the last thing I want to do is fight with you. So just forget I said anything."

Bryan nodded. "Fine, but will you tell me something? It's been bugging me for a while and I just need an answer. Then I promise I'll leave you alone and you can go on ignoring me."

I shrugged. "Depends."

He chuckled, "I thought you would say that, but I want to know why I wasn't enough for you? What does Chase have that I don't have?"

"Nothing, Bryan, there were a lot of things that went into my choice."

"It was your choice, right?"

That made me mad. Was he saying I couldn't make decisions for myself?

"Of course, it was my choice! Just like sending your mom to Texas is your choice!" I covered my mouth right when I said that, wishing I could take the words back.

Anger flashed in his eyes. "I might send her. It's for her benefit, believe me."

"You don't think she'd be more comfortable with you?"

"Comfort and getting healthy again don't always coexist. Besides, I don't have to explain to you. It doesn't matter." He turned to walk away and I grabbed his hand and turned him around.

"Bryan, what is it?"

"You won't understand." I grabbed his hand and he jerked it away.

"Then please explain it to me." I could tell that I was pleading now, but it got to him. The wave of anger was replaced with defeat. In that moment, I broke through Bryan's hard shell and he broke down, tears beginning to fill his eyes.

"It hurts me! Every day to see her in pain, day in and day out, and knowing that I can't do anything to help her. She's all alone; she won't talk to me anymore. I can't continue to see her going through that. It's getting harder and harder for me to take care of her. I'm just afraid that if I don't get someone to help her while I'm still fighting that maybe one day I'm not going to want to fight anymore. She keeps slipping further and further away from me, and there is nothing I can do to stop it. I'm sick of feeling alone. Ever since you left, that hole gets bigger and bigger. I'm at a breaking point, Katie. I don't know what else to turn to and I don't know who to turn to."

When he broke, I broke. I closed the distance between us and wrapped my arms around his waist.

"You can turn to me. You know I'll always be here for you, Bryan." I kissed his shoulder; it took every ounce of strength in me to stop there. We stood there for a couple of minutes. I realized I was hugging him, but his arms still weren't around me. I could feel my eyes getting watery. "I'm sorry, Bryan, for everything. You deserve better. I made a huge mistake by leading Chase on, but I couldn't help it. I know that's a bad excuse, but I feel like this is my fault. Like I—"

"Katie! You didn't do anything wrong." Suddenly his arms were around my waist and he pulled me to his chest and whispered in my ear. "You did everything right." We stared into each other's eyes for a few seconds before we slowly started inching towards each other. Right before our lips were about to touch, my phone started to ring. I felt my heart drop all the way to my feet. I pulled away, clearing my head. Bryan let out a long, irritated sigh. I pulled my phone out of my back pocket and saw that the caller ID said 'Chase.' I looked over at Bryan.

"I have to take this."

He crossed his arms over his chest. "He's always in the way." Bryan walked over to me and put his hand behind my neck and kissed my forehead gently; then looked at me once before turning to walk away.

I looked down at my phone, then back up at Bryan walking away. Suddenly, my mind seemed like it was on autopilot.

I didn't know what I was doing until I dropped my phone on the ground and called out, "Bryan!"

He turned around just in time to catch me before I ran into him. I put my hands on his face and kissed him with everything I had left in me. After a couple of seconds, he pushed me away and restrained me with his hands.

"Please, don't Katie. It will only make it harder when you leave. I'm not going to be the other guy."

"Bryan, don't do this. I'm begging you. I need you." He pulled me to his chest and wrapped his arms around me.

"Sometimes what we want and what we need are two different things. The hardest thing to figure out in life is learning which one is which." He kissed me on the cheek, slowly. When he pulled away, we heard laughing from inside the house. We both looked towards the open window that overlooked the side of the house and sure enough, there were the twins and Greg. I looked over at Scotty who was making kissy faces, while Sam had turned his back towards us as he rubbed his hands up and down his back making it look like he was making out with someone. Greg was laughing before he yelled, "Get a room!"

I blushed and Bryan chuckled as he said, "I should have known they would be watching." I looked up at him and laughed.

A few seconds later, the twins and Greg were standing in front of us. For a second, none of them said anything, but then Scotty broke the silence. "Well, I'm happy to announce that I just won $20 thanks to that little kiss you two lovebirds just shared." I blushed again.

Bryan shook his head. "How did you manage to win that?" Even though Bryan directed this question at Scotty, Sam took the liberty of answering it.

"Scott said that within the next week, Bryan would make a move on Katie or vice versa. While Greg and I—" he put his hand to his chest— "said that Bryan wouldn't have the nerve to make a move for a while, so nothing would happen for a month or two."

I crossed my arms over my chest. "So either way, you guys thought I would end up cheating on my boyfriend? Oh, geez, I did just cheat on my boyfriend."

Greg chuckled. "Well, to be honest, we didn't know how long you and your little boyfriend would last, but…" When the boys laughed and I didn't, they got the message that what they just said wasn't funny. When that realization came over Greg's face, he said, "Katie, we're kidding. We just…I don't know…we're all kind of rooting for you and Bryan." After he said this, I looked over at Bryan who was looking at me. He smiled weakly at me, but I could see the humor in his eyes. I shoved him a little before walking inside.

The next morning I knew what I had to do, who I had to see. I climbed into my car and drove over to

Bryan's house. When I got there, Bryan's truck was gone, but I guessed that was for the best, because he wasn't who I was here to see. I didn't know what drove me to come here, I just felt like I had to. As I slowly walked up to the house, my stomach started to fill with knots. I started to pray that God would let the words that needed to be said flow freely out of my mouth. When I got to the door, I tapped on it. A few minutes later, the door opened slowly and Bryan's mom was standing there. Her blonde hair was pulled up into a messy ponytail and she looked confused. I looked down at her hands and saw that she was holding a beer bottle. By the looks of it, it wasn't her first one of the day.

I smiled. "Hi, Julie." She just looked at me. It was almost as if she was trying to put the pieces of a puzzle together. "It's me, Katie."

She shook her head, "I'm sorry, I don't remember..." Her voice trailed off.

"No, that's fine. I just wanted to talk to you." She staggered backwards before taking a big gulp of her drink, then dropped the bottle on the floor. She turned and walked into the kitchen. I took that as her invitation to enter. I slowly crept into the house. When I reached the kitchen, I saw her reach into the refrigerator and pull out another cold one. I sighed.

"How many of those have you had today?" She just looked at me, then down by the trash can. I followed her gaze and saw two bottles leaning against each other in the trash can and three around it. I figured that by her third one she was too out of it to get them into the trashcan. So adding those together, plus the one she had finished at the door, she was working on her seventh. I clasped my hands and said, "Okay, Julie, I have an idea. Let's have some water." I walked over to her and grabbed the bottle out of her hands. I didn't realize taking a beer from an alcoholic is like taking a pacifier from a tired baby. Suddenly her confused gaze turned into a glare, causing me to take a step back. Then she was yelling.

"Get your hands off of me!" She paused to take a deep breath. "Why are you here?" Then another breath. "You think you can barge into my house and take my drinks!" Then an even deeper breath. "Go buy your own!"

I drew my own deep breath. "Julie, you need to stop drinking. It's not good for you or for Bryan. He is trying to help you, so at least meet him halfway."

"You think you can steal my beer, then tell me what I'm doing wrong with my boy. You have no idea what we've been through. Just get out." Her breathing was becoming ragged. I walked over to her and put my hands on her shoulders.

"Let me help you to the couch."

"Get your hands off me!" I saw her arm reach back on the table and grab an empty bottle. She then grabbed the collar of my jacket and held the bottle over her head; then before I knew what was happening, she swung. In the middle of her swing, I heard, "Mom, no!" Then I was pushed to the floor. I hadn't been hit with the bottle, but I heard the pieces of it fall to the kitchen tile.

I looked up at Julie as she whispered, "I'm going to bed." She slowly walked to the couch and curled up on it. She didn't even realize what she had just done. I could tell how bad off she was just by that. I looked around to see what she could have hit with the bottle, and then it registered. The familiar voice. I turned and saw Bryan lying on the floor.

"Bryan!" I crawled over to him and rolled him on his back. He was holding the side of his face and looking at me.

"First my hand, now this. If I have to save you one more time, I don't know if I will make it."

"Let me look at you." I grabbed his hand and pulled it away from his face. There was blood everywhere. I knew I wouldn't be able to see how bad it was until I cleaned the blood off. I walked over to the sink and got the dish towel. I poured water on it and went to kneel over Bryan. He just looked at me while I gently dabbed all the blood away. I frowned every time he winced in pain; pain that I caused. When all the blood was gone, there were many scrapes, but the ones I was concerned about were two big gashes on the side of his face.

"I need to take you to the hospital." He grabbed my hand when I was about to stand up.

"No, I'm fine. Katie please, they'll take her away."

"We need to get that cleaned up."

He sighed. "Your dad has a first aid kit." I rolled my eyes, because I knew where that meant we were going.

When we got back to my house, I was going to help Bryan out of the truck, but he was out of the truck before I had even closed my door. The whole ride over, I made him hold a towel on his face to prevent him from bleeding to death. He laughed about it the whole way here because he felt weak having to hold a towel to his face. His blood was starting to soak through the thick towel. I sighed. If anything happened to him, I knew it was because of me. As we started walking to the door, the golf cart came around the corner with Frankie and the twins. The twins jumped out when they saw the bloody towel.

Scotty ran over and pulled Bryan's hand away from the cut so he could see it. "Dang, Bryan! I didn't know Katie abused you!" Bryan pushed him lightly, but then Sam was there.

"I knew you were whipped, but I didn't know you got whipped!"

Bryan laughed sarcastically. "Ha-ha, very funny. Katie didn't do this." Then the twins started asking him questions about who did it and why he didn't fight back. Bryan just shook his head, not wanting to answer. I was about to say something when I heard

Frankie walk up and grab the twins by the shoulders.

"Come on, boys. The carts loaded, no thanks to you. Let's get back to work. Let the boy be!" He pulled the twins to the golf cart. By the time the golf cart pulled around to the backyard, the twins were already laughing about something else. When we got inside, I looked around for my dad, but then saw him through the window down by the vineyard. I led Bryan to the table and had to force him to sit down. He said he could clean it up himself, but I refused to let him. Once he sat down, I walked over to the medicine cabinet and pulled out my dad's first aid kit, then sat in the chair next to him and opened it up.

"I can clean it up myself, you don't have to."

"I know, but I want to. It's my fault you got hurt anyway."

He rolled his eyes. "I'm glad it was me and not you."

I took out gauze and started dabbing all the left-over blood away, revealing the gash marks even clearer. Then he added, "We both know I'm the only one who can pull this look off." He joked as I studied the cuts. Well, he was right, he didn't need stitches. They weren't too deep, but they were deep enough for me to feel really bad.

"Why am I always the one that hurts you?"

He just laughed, "Cuz you do what you want, even if you shouldn't." After he said that, I poured alcohol on the gauze and dabbed his cuts to make sure they didn't get infected. As I did that, he winced.

"I guess I do that a lot... I mess up everything, don't I?"

He shrugged. "Not everything." I pushed the gauze harder on his face and he pulled away. "Dang, Katie!"

"I did mess us up."

He sighed, "Katie, can we just not talk about it for one conversation."

"I won't talk about it if you tell me that you don't think about what we could have been."

He looked down. "Of course, I think about it, but you shouldn't because ultimately, it was your choice." He looked back up at me. I leaned in to kiss him and right before we kissed, he pushed my hand holding the gauze away and stood up. I watched him walk to the backyard. I looked down at my hands and threw the gauze in the trash. After a couple of minutes, I walked outside to join him on the back porch. I saw him leaning against the railing. It was hard to miss the blood stain on his bright yellow shirt. I started to walk over to him and rested my hands on the railing next to his. He looked over at me, hesitated and then walked over to the other side of the porch and leaned against the rail again. I looked over at him with a confused expression on my face; then took a few steps toward him, but froze when he said, "Don't take another step." He looked up at me and his eyes were saying something completely different.

"Why?"

"Because I don't want to get between you and Chase. And every time you're close to me, I want to kiss you, but I can't." He looked down.

"I thought that you had moved on. I mean, you have Rachel now."

"Rachel was only a distraction to get my mind off you. When I realized it didn't work, I let her know."

"But why would you want to kiss me if you don't want to be the other guy?" He seemed to hesitate for a moment, like he was thinking about what to say because he didn't want to say what was really on his mind. I could tell he gave up trying because he took a deep breath and looked away from me and out to the vineyard.

"I said I didn't want to be the other guy, but that's only because, I want to be the only guy." He looked at me, then walked over and sat down on one of the chairs. I was about to say something when my dad walked up.

"Hey, Bryan, wasn't expecting to see you here. Whoa, what happened to your face?" My dad glanced over at me and I rolled my eyes. Bryan just shrugged.

"I ran into something. Can you take me home, sir?"

My dad dropped the bag of berries he had gathered in the vineyard as he said, "Sure, bud. Let's go."

Bryan looked over at me and nodded, then walked

away with my dad. I sighed and looked out onto the acres of land we owned, and was still trying to make myself wake up from the dream I was in. What Bryan had just said seemed unreal. I had been secretly hoping he still wanted me. Now that I knew the truth, it changed everything.

CHAPTER 19

I woke up the next morning after a restless night feeling like I had only slept for about five minutes. All I could think about was what Bryan had said. I needed to talk to him, I had to fix this. I called him once and it went to his voice mail. The second time, after the second ring, it went to voicemail. The third time he answered, then hung up without saying a word. He wanted to play games? Well, then I could, too. I walked downstairs after getting dressed. I was about to walk out the back door when I saw my dad staring at me from the kitchen table.

"What's the big rush, kiddo?"

"Please, no questions. I'm in a hurry. Did Bryan come to work this morning?"

My dad looked at me puzzled. "No, he called and said he needed a day off. Since when are you interested in his work schedule? I thought you two were—" He motioned through the air.

"We are."

"Okay? You know what, forget it. I give up trying to decode the female mind." He laughed as I rolled my eyes and walked out the door. I started my car and drove over to Bryan's house. When I passed his driveway and his truck wasn't there, I slammed on my brakes. I didn't know where else he would have gone. I laid my head against the steering wheel before a thought came to me. Where else would he go for a day off? Somewhere he could really be alone; a place where nobody would find him. Nobody except me. The waterfall.

Now that I knew where I was headed, I got there much faster. I smiled when I saw his truck at the top of the hill. I parked right next to his truck and climbed out. When I made it to the waterfall, I tried to jump through as fast as I could into the cave to avoid getting soaked, but that was a lost cause. I was still completely soaked. I pushed the hair out of my face and caught the eyes of a surprised Bryan. I smiled at his soaked tan shorts and simple purple button-down shirt with rolled up sleeves. The shirt was halfway open revealing a blue v-neck. He just stared at me, then finally broke the silence.

"What are you doing here?" He refused to make eye contact with me and every time I tried to hold his eyes, he would look away.

'I wouldn't even be here if you would have just taken my call. Why are you ignoring me?!"

He shrugged and simply said, "I left my phone at home." Then he went back to strumming his guitar.

"Oh, that explains it, I——"

"I mean, don't get me wrong. If I would have brought it with me, I wouldn't have answered your call anyway." He smiled slightly.

"Why would you tell me that? Did you wake up this morning and just think of all the ways you could hurt me today?"

He abruptly stopped strumming and set his guitar down and stood up quickly. "Me? Hurt you? You've got to be joking. You aren't the victim here, Katie. You never were."

"At least I take your phone calls."

"I never call you!"

"Well, I would take your phone calls if you did. I wouldn't ignore you."

"Cheating and ignoring are two completely different things. Last time I checked, ignoring is the higher road to cheating."

I walked closer to him. "I didn't cheat."

He grunted, then walked up close to me, "Really? Then look me right in the eyes and swear on my life that you never kissed him. That you never had feelings for him and that you never wanted something more." I looked down at my feet, I couldn't meet his eyes. I felt like a little kid that got caught with her hand in a cookie jar.

"That's not fair."

Bryan took a few steps back. "You cheated on me, and I'm the unfair one? You know what? You're such a hypocrite! Do you even hear yourself right now?" What he said startled me. Nobody had ever talked to me like that. I sat down on a rock sticking out from the side of the cave. "Besides, we kissed yesterday; so technically, you cheated on him, too."

"You're right, this is my fault. I'm treating you unfairly and I'm treating Chase unfairly." I hid my face in my hands. I heard him sigh and suddenly his arm was around me and he was sitting next to me.

"Well, at least you're figuring that out now." He chuckled and I pushed against him.

"Why do you still care anyway?"

I felt him shrug. "Love didn't just go away because you broke my heart. It's still there. I'm always going to be here for you, Katie."

I leaned into his shoulder.

After a couple minutes he stood up. "I'm sorry, I...I can't. I'll be here for you, on the other side of the cave." The smile I love came to his lips.

"You make it so hard for me to be happy with Chase. I can't keep lying to myself about that. I want you all to myself, but..."

"But you want Chase."

I nodded.

He sighed. "Well I'm not going to wait in the wings forever."

"Tell me how to choose because right now, single sounds a lot better than being between two guys."

He laughed. "I can't tell you that. But I do know that at one point in your life, you have to decide who you are, and who you want to be. Once you know that, then you see who helps bring that person out of you."

I sighed. "You make it sound so easy."

"Well, it's not going to be." He laughed. "Listen, the last thing I want you to do is pick someone because you feel sorry for them. So just promise me something, okay?"

I nodded.

"Promise me that no matter who you pick, it's what you really want."

"I promise." I looked into his eyes and smiled when his lips pulled back into a smile.

"Katie." He said my name gently, so gently that I barely heard it. "What do you want?" I just shook my head, unable to say anything. "Katie, it's a simple question. What do you want? Who do you want?"

I looked at Bryan. "It's not that simple."

"Seriously? That's the easiest question you're ever going to have to answer. What do you want, Katie?!"

"It doesn't matter what I want!"

"It's your life, so of course, it matters!"

I shook my head and before I knew it, I was yelling. "You want to know what I want! I want my parents to get back together. I want us to be a family again. I want my friends back. I want everything to go back to how it was before Lucas died! But you know that's never going to happen! No matter how hard I wish for it, Lucas is still dead, my parents are never going to get back together, and my friends...I don't even know those people anymore!"

"So you want everything to go back to how it was

before you met me? Even before you met Chase?"

I took a deep breath, "If that's what it takes."

Bryan ran a hand through his hair and walked toward the back of the cave. Before he picked up his guitar, he looked back at me. "Well, I'm sorry, but Lucas is still dead. Nothing's changed. But I won't contact you, or talk to you, so it will be like before you ever met me." He looked away from me and started playing his guitar while tears poured down his face.

Tears started overflowing in my eyes.

"Bryan, come on! I didn't mean it, I—"

When he didn't look up at me, I'd had enough. I ran out of the waterfall and into my car. I drove as fast as I could to the nearest parking lot and parked. I laid my head on the steering wheel and cried as the four words haunted me. What did I want?

CHAPTER 20

I ran inside the house after getting home from the waterfall, and went straight upstairs to my room. I started shoving my clothes in my suitcase while trying to hold back the tears.

"What are you doing?" I looked up to see my dad standing in the doorway.

"I have to go. Chase will be home tomorrow and my week is up."

"It's summer. You don't have to leave." My dad walked over to my suitcase and put his hand on top of it so I couldn't put anything else in there. "You just came back, kiddo. I don't want to see you leave again." I wrapped my arms around my dad's waist.

"You won't, I promise. I'll be back. Soon." He sighed and picked up my suitcase, then quickly walked downstairs and put it in my car. As he looked down at me, I was in the middle of wiping my eyes.

"Does your leaving have anything to do with Bryan?"

"Dad, I don't want to talk about him. I can't talk to him."

"Promise me one thing."

"Anything, Dad." My mood was instantly lifted when his face was filled with a big smile.

"Don't wait two months to come see me again."

I laughed and rolled my eyes as I said, "Bye, dad, I love you."

"Are you sure you don't want some dinner first?"

I shook my head. "Goodbye, dad."

When I entered my neighborhood, I drove down Chase's street to see if he was home early, not expecting him to be. But as I passed his house, I saw him climbing out of his Hummer in black shorts with a plain white T-shirt. I smiled as I stopped my car and ran over to him. A big smile came to his face and he pulled me into his arms. I laid my head on his chest, and smiled when I heard his heart beat in sync with mine. I looked up at him as he said, "I missed you so much."

I smiled and responded, "Let's grab lunch tomorrow. I really have to get home."

He nodded. "For sure." Then he leaned down and kissed me slowly. I was smiling all the way back to my car.

When I got home, I knew something was up. Because when I walked in the front door, my mother and Mike were sitting on the couch like they were waiting for me to come home. When I walked a little closer, I noticed that two more people were there, Mr. and Mrs. Masterson, Lucas's parents. All four adults' eyes were red like they had been crying. I was hesitant as I entered the living room. All eyes were on me. I settled my gaze upon my mom.

"What's going on?" My mom looked over at Mike and wiped her eyes before answering.

"Honey, we have to talk to you." I sat on the only empty chair left. My mom looked towards the Masterson's and nodded. I looked towards Mrs. Masterson as she began to talk.

"Sweetheart, we haven't been entirely honest with you about Lucas."

I looked at her confused. "What do you mean?"

Mrs. Masterson looked over at her husband as he continued for her. "We were trying to give you time to move on, so the news wouldn't be so hard on you." He looked at me for a second while I put the pieces together in my mind.

"You know how Lucas died." It wasn't a question, but rather a statement. I kept my gaze on Mr. Masterson as he continued.

"We wanted to keep the story away from the press. The police called a halt on the investigation; not because it wasn't going anywhere, but because we already knew what happened." He paused for a second to hold back tears before continuing. "Lucas...Lucas was dying even before his death. He was diagnosed with non-treatable Leukemia. They were keeping him on medication so it didn't show on the outside as much."

I shook my head. "No, he was perfectly healthy. He was fine. No, he wasn't sick. Even if he did have Leukemia, it couldn't just kill him that fast, something drastic would have happened." I could feel the tears filling my eyes. Lucas was going to die anyway.

Mrs. Masterson continued on with tears running down her face. "The only thing drastic that happened was the choice that Lucas made. The taking of his life... suicide."

My breathing was becoming heavier and heavier. "Why would he...that doesn't sound like him. What would—?"

My mom put her hand on my knee. "He left this in his wallet." I took the piece of paper from her and unfolded it:

Mom and Dad,
Do not blame yourselves for what I have done. Everything happens for a reason. Please know that this is what I wanted. Why drag out death? I lived every moment to the fullest. I lived like I was dying, because on the inside, I was. I love you both. Thank you for filling every moment with pure happiness and love. I love you both so deeply.
Love,
Your son, Lucas

Katie,
I know that this will be unexpected. I always told you that I would never hurt you, but this is for the best. I was diagnosed with Leukemia and didn't tell you because I knew by me telling you, it wouldn't change

anything. I wanted you to remember me happy and healthy, not sick and dying. Remember the singing conventions, the dirt bike races, remember the good times. I know you always said that you could take care of yourself. Well, now is your chance to prove it. This was the best solution I could come up with because I was not going to let you watch me die. I couldn't stand the thought of you sitting around knowing that my time was running out. Writing this note, I realize that you only get one chance at life, and you can't waste the little moments that matter the most. I want you to find someone who makes you feel alive, and someone who will always be there for you, because I couldn't be. I love you more than life itself. I'm sorry I never got the chance to prove that to you.

Forever yours,

Lucas

I had been bawling since I read my name on the paper. I threw the paper down and ran out of the house. I ran to the graveyard where Lucas had been buried and quickly found his tombstone. I sat down in front of it and ran my hands over it still crying. I kept saying, 'I'm sorry, I'm sorry.' But I didn't know what for. A part of me felt like I was the one who killed him. He drove his car into that tree so I wouldn't have to watch him die. I don't know how long I sat there staring at the gravestone, but it was long enough because I jumped when I heard someone speak behind me.

"You know it's not good to sit in a graveyard all by yourself." I turned around to see Bryan standing there with a single rose in his hand. I wiped the tears from my eyes. He smiled then shifted his weight a little. "Almost forgot." He pulled out a packet of tissue and handed them to me.

"How did you find me?"

"Your mom called your dad after you were gone for two hours. All of the guys were at your dad's house to watch the big baseball game. He told us what was happening and I got worried, so volunteered to come find you."

He came and sat down beside me. "I promised I would always be here for you, and that outweighed the no contact thing." He put his arm around me when I started crying again, and I leaned my head into his shoulder. "Why are you out here all alone anyway?"

"Lucas…it turns out, he killed himself. He was diagnosed with Leukemia, and he didn't want me to see him…die. So he thought this…was better."

"Katie, I know how hard death can be. Trust me. But as time passes, you see it in a whole new way."

I looked up at him. "How did you get over your dad being gone?"

He sighed and looked at the ground. "Well, it took time, but I think the funeral helped a little bit. Seeing all those people who were going to miss him; it helped me see I wasn't alone."

I stood up abruptly. I walked a couple of feet away and turned around when Bryan asked, "What did I say?"

I shook my head. "I didn't go, okay! I pulled up to the church, but chickened out. I didn't have the strength to say goodbye. I knew that if I walked in that church, then his death turned to reality, and I couldn't handle that. I still wake up thinking that he's going to walk through my front door and wrap me in his arms. But he's not going to!"

Bryan walked over to me and pulled me to his chest. "Hey, it's okay." He rubbed my back trying to calm me down. "It's not too late. You can say goodbye when you're ready. The funeral isn't the only time." I pulled away and looked him in the eyes. He handed me the single rose, then nodded toward the grave. I gently took the rose and walked over to the gravestone. When I got there, I fell to my knees.

"Hey Luke, I finally understand why you had so many doctors' appointments. You told me it was for all your colds, but now I see the real reason. You were very sick. I'm sorry I couldn't be there to hold your hand in the hospital. I wish you would have told me so I would have had the chance to do that. I'm sorry I haven't visited, much less said goodbye. I just want to say what I never had the chance to say. I love you." I set the rose on top of the gravestone and kissed the edge of the stone. "Goodbye." I laid my hand on top of it, then turned and walked toward Bryan.

He smiled. "Let's get you back home." He turned to leave.

"Wait."

He turned around. "What?"

"I was so mean to you earlier, I'm—"

"Forget it, it didn't happen." He smiled. "Can we go now?"

"There is something I should have done a long time ago." I put one of my hands on his shoulder and the other on the back of his head and kissed him with all the passion and love left in me. Lucas was right. I only had one chance at life, and I knew what I wanted, who I wanted.

CHAPTER 21

I walked through my front door at 1:30 in the morning after leaving the graveyard. I was hand-in-hand with Bryan. Let's just say that my mom wasn't very happy with me. When we walked in the door, she was sitting in the same chair she was hours before just staring at the door.

I heard Bryan whisper, "You sure this is safe?" I lightly hit him in the stomach, then couldn't help but smile when I saw him beaming.

My mom walked over to us, but wouldn't make eye contact with Bryan. She looked at me and said, "Can I speak to you for a minute?"

I nodded and walked into the office and left Bryan standing by the door.

"What, Mom?" I looked over at her.

"Is that the boy from the wedding? Why is he here? How do you think Chase would feel if—?"

"Mom, this isn't about Chase. It's about what makes me happy. And he's here because I wouldn't let him drive all the way home tonight. So I told him he can stay here." I looked up at my mom.

"It's my choice whether he can stay here tonight or not!"

"Mom! It's late. I'm not going to lose another

boyfriend because he was driving home too late. Why don't you like him? Why are you so hung up on me dating Chase? The truth is, Mom, I tried to force myself to be happy with Chase. But with Bryan, it comes natural. You know what I realized? The only reason I even agreed to be Chase's girlfriend was because of you. It got to the point where I was choosing between living with you and living with Dad. And honestly, if you aren't going to even try to like Bryan, then I would rather go live with Dad." I sighed and walked out of the office. Bryan just looked at me with an uncomfortable look on his face.

I didn't wait for my mom to come out of the office. I was determined to finally get everything I wanted. I grabbed Bryan's hand and dragged him upstairs to the guest room right beside mine. When we got in the room, Bryan finally spoke.

"I don't want you getting in fights with your mom over me. I would have been fine driving home." I smiled and went over to wrap my arms around his neck and bury my head into his shoulder.

"I know. I don't know what got into me."

Bryan laughed and said, "Your stubbornness." I pulled back and punched him lightly in the chest. He grabbed my hand and kissed it, then pulled me closer and kissed me lightly. After a couple of seconds, I pulled away.

"Oh, tomorrow might be highly dangerous for you."

Bryan's face twisted into a confused look. "Why?"

"I'm supposed to be meeting Chase for lunch and I want you there with me when I tell him about us."

Bryan smiled and said, "So should I wear a bullet proof vest?"

I chuckled as I responded, "I don't think that will protect you." I stood up on the tips of my toes and kissed him before whispering "I love you" in his ear. I started to walk out the door when he grabbed my hand and said, "I love you more."

I smiled and said, "Goodnight."

The next morning, I woke up, stretched, and climbed out of bed to see a truck I recognized in the driveway. Then I remembered that Bryan had stayed the night. I quickly got dressed and knocked on his door. When nobody answered, I walked into his room. He was lying down on the bed, still sleeping. He was on his back, with one hand draped over his stomach while the other was sprawled out in the opposite direction. I smiled as I went over to wake him up. I shook his arm lightly and called his name, but he didn't wake up. So I went to plan B, I got a pillow and threw it at his head. He sprung up and laughed when he saw me standing there.

He looked over to where the pillow had landed and said, "Cute, very cute." Then he reached behind him and threw his pillow at me. I gasped as it hit me in the arm.

"That's not fair! I threw the pillow at you to wake

you up, sleepy head." I smiled at him as he chuckled and ran a hand through his hair.

"Well, now that I'm awake, will you tell me why you rudely woke me up?" He smiled.

"We have to leave in 10 minutes."

"Why?" He responded with a clueless look on his face.

"We have to go meet Chase for lunch."

"Oh, right." Bryan rolled on his side, before pulling himself up to sit on the bed.

I realized he was only wearing his boxers, so I walked over to the foot of the bed and picked up his jeans from the floor. I threw them on the bed beside him. He looked up and smiled at me as he stood up and slid his jeans on. He looked up at me and said, "I don't have time to go out and buy a bullet proof vest, so hopefully he has really bad aim."

I laughed as I walked over to him and slid my hands around his waist as I laid my head on his chest. I felt him rest his chin on the top of my head before gently kissing it. We stood there for a few seconds before I pulled away. I slid my hands from his waist up to his chest. I rested one hand on his chest while I put the other on the side of his face to guide his lips to mine. I kissed him lightly before whispering, "Everything will be fine."

I pulled away as I reached down on the bed to hand him his shirt. He pulled on his black tank top before putting on his white button down shirt. His jeans were faded painter jeans and he was wearing his black boots. I quickly told him I had an extra toothbrush in my bathroom and that I would meet him downstairs in the truck.

When we were on our way to the diner, I looked over at Bryan and saw that his hands were gripping the steering wheel so tightly that his knuckles were turning white. I cleared my throat and asked, "Is everything alright?"

He looked over at me and smiled. "Yeah, of course. It's just I feel sort of weird going to this lunch. Should I just wait in the car? I mean this guy likes you and isn't so fond of me."

"No, I need you in there. Chase will understand."

He shrugged. "I hope you're right."

When we walked into the diner, I saw the back of Chase's head. I started to walk over to him and could tell that Bryan was following far behind me. When I got to Chase, I tapped him on the shoulder. When he turned around, he had a huge smile on his face and pulled me into a hug.

"I'm so happy to see you-" Then Bryan walked up and Chase finished, "-with him." Chase looked over at me and I saw a wave of sadness followed by a look of betrayal flash across his face.

"Chase, let me explain." He didn't take his eyes off Bryan. I felt Bryan shift uncomfortably by my side and slide his hand lightly around my waist, then I felt him relax a little more.

"Explain what? That you lied to me? You said you didn't go to your dad's for him. You said you didn't have feelings for him anymore. I told you this would happen, Katie, I knew this would happen. Every time that I feel like I'm finally enough for you, there he is, always in the way."

"Chase, you're my best friend. If anyone should understand this, it's you. I never wanted to hurt you. It just happened. I didn't go there for him. I promise."

Chase still wouldn't look at me. "I understand that, Katie, but it doesn't change anything. Look, I honestly do understand that he's the one, for now; but you never even gave me a chance to show you that I could have been, too. But now, now I'm just a pathetic guy standing in your way." He stepped around me.

"Chase, wait——"

He suddenly turned around and finally looked at me.

"No, Katie! I'm through waiting. You made me wait when I first wanted to take you out, but you let him the first day you met him. You made me wait to kiss you because you weren't ready; but when you were with him, you were all puckered up. You made me wait every time I was ready to take the next step. Then when you would go to your dad's, all of a sudden you're ready for a relationship. So no, I'm not waiting anymore. Because every time I wait, I get hurt and I'm tired of it."

Then as fast as he had turned around, he was out

the door. I couldn't believe what just happened. I looked up at Bryan who was studying me carefully. He knew he didn't have to say anything as he pulled me to his chest. I cried lightly into his shoulder and to help keep my embarrassment to a minimum, he guided me to his car and just sat there comforting me without saying a word.

I woke up the next morning groggy, almost confused as to what had happened the day before. I had a big spot on my pillow from where my tears had dried during the night. I never wanted Bryan to see me cry like that, especially if it was tears for another guy and especially Chase. After I pulled myself out of bed, I went to the room that Bryan had used the night before, but it was empty. As I walked back to my room, I was starting to wonder where he had gone, but I figured he was downstairs or driving home.

When I got to my room, I walked over to the window to look outside. The outside world was so peaceful and bright that it looked almost surreal. It had been a long time since I had seen the world this way. Despite everything that happened yesterday, I was happy. It hit me that because I finally let go of Lucas, I saw the world in a different light. No longer was I looking at the world through foggy eyes that could only see part of the picture. Now I was seeing it through clear eyes. I finally saw that big picture and knew that everything was going to be okay.

As I started to back away from the window, I wondered why Bryan left without even saying goodbye.

But I quickly shook it off, because it didn't matter. I turned to my closet and as I was about to open it, something caught my eye. It was glistening. I walked over to it and saw the heart necklace that Chase had given me before he left for his grandparent's house and under it was a note.

> K,
>
> *After I brought you home yesterday, I thought it was better if I left to check on my mom and everything. You were pretty out of it when I carried you upstairs. I saw this necklace on the ground before I left and didn't want you to lose it. I love you.*
>
> *Call me whenever,*
>
> *Bryan*

CHAPTER 22

I rolled my window down as I was driving on the now familiar back road to get to Bryan's house after school. My mind started to think about how everything changed when my senior year started, yet it almost seemed like everything was the same. I couldn't believe it was already the fifth week of school. I had tests to study for, but I was happy I had Bryan to study with. When I got to his house, I walked inside without knocking. His house was beginning to feel like a second home to me. His mother was starting to get better with her drinking. She had spent all of August proving to Bryan that she didn't need to go to rehab and when school started, he finally believed her. Their house was cleaner now that she was sober. Everything was in its place and you could almost see the floors glisten when the sun streamed in through the dustless windows. I walked into the kitchen and saw that Bryan was already filling two glasses with sweet tea, just like he did every day we used his house to study. I walked over to him and wrapped my arms around him from behind and he chuckled.

"Is that you, Rachel?"

"Bryan!" I slapped his shoulder lightly and then couldn't help but laugh. He said he was kidding before leaning down to kiss me. We walked into his living room where he already had his homework sprawled out on the coffee table. Heading in first, I cleared off a section of the table so he had somewhere to put the drinks down. Then I stood there waiting for him to sit down. When he did, I sat down beside him and leaned against him. It was almost as if our bodies were one. We fit perfectly together. I pulled my calendar from my backpack to see what my homework assignment was and noticed the date. September 14. Lucas' birthday. I looked up at Bryan and even though my facial expression was blank, he knew something was wrong.

"What's up?"

"Lucas would have turned 18 today." Bryan took a deep breath beside me.

"Sometimes I wonder why it was him that was sick and not me. And why did he think he needed to kill himself. Did I do something wrong?"

Bryan's grip tightened around my waist. "You didn't do anything wrong. Do you think Lucas would want you asking yourself all these questions? He didn't give up his life for you to waste yours wondering." I felt Bryan kiss me on top of the head and I smiled as I rested my head on his shoulder. I hated how right he was, but I knew deep down I had known that was the answer. I just needed someone to tell me. We sat there in silence for a few minutes. I didn't know what Bryan was thinking about, but I wasn't sure if I wanted to know. I was content with just sitting there with Bryan's arms wrapped around me.

We had been studying for a couple of hours when I heard Bryan's mom, Julie, walk through the door. She had finally come to her senses and now works at my dad's vineyard instead of Bryan having to work, as well as go to school. She doesn't actually have to do any of the picking. She works in the factory that my dad built at the end of the summer that is located about five minutes away from our house. She is in charge of the shipments. She oversees the boxes that come from my dad's vineyard to the factory and the boxes that have to be shipped from the factory to various warehouses all over the world. All the guys miss Bryan up at the vineyard, but we hang out with them from time to time; and Bryan visits the vineyard and even works when they need an extra hand with something. When she walked through the front door, she saw Bryan and I studying on the couch.

She smiled and quietly whispered, "Sorry, didn't mean to interrupt your studying."

I smiled back, "No, it's fine. I was just leaving."

I looked over at Bryan who had just risen from the couch. He walked over to his mom and kissed her on the cheek. "Hey, Mom."

"Hey, Bry." She gave him a hug, then walking into the kitchen, pulled out a bottle of water from the fridge before heading to the kitchen table to sit down.

I gathered all my things from the table and threw them into my backpack. I looked over at Bryan who was waiting patiently by the door to walk me to my car. As I approached the door, he gently pulled the door open as he took my hand with his free one. We walked to my car in silence. He opened the driver's side door for me and I threw my bag in the passenger seat before turning back to look at him. Before I could say anything, he pulled me into a hug. I laughed before putting my hands on the back of his neck and kissing him. I locked my fingers in his hair feeling our bodies mold together. We pulled away from each other, but kept our hands clasped together. I looked down at my watch and saw it was 9:00 o'clock.

I still had a 30 minute drive back to my house. I looked at Bryan and said I should get going.

He nodded, "Call me when you get home, so I know you made it there okay."

I smiled and leaned up to kiss him. Before I got in my car I heard him say, "I love you, Katie."

I turned to look at him. "I love you, too, Bryan. I'll call you later."

When I got home, I pulled out my phone to text Bryan that I had made it safely. I also said I would call him after I got in my room. When I walked through the front door, the aroma that engulfed the house reminded me of one of the Italian places down the street from our house, Lasagna Garden. It made my mouth water just thinking of that restaurant. I walked into the kitchen to find my mother making homemade lasagna. My eyebrows pulled together. Why was she making lasagna this late at night? Before I could ask her why, she looked up at me and asked, "How was studying at Bryan's?"

I nodded as I said fine. She looked like she had something on her mind. "Katie, I just hope you guys are really studying over at his house. I also want to make sure that things aren't too serious between you two. You have to think of your education right now. You have plenty of time to worry about boys later."

I laughed and she looked up at me. "Mom, Bryan and I do study, and he's not just some boy. I can honestly tell you right now that he could be the one."

She smiled at me. "Whatever you say. I hope you know what you're doing. Because right now from the sidelines, it looks like you're going one way, and then you turn around and change directions."

"I wish I could say I knew exactly what I was doing." I walked over to the stove where the sauce was bubbling a little and pulled the spoon up from the pot to taste the sauce. "This is really good. I'm impressed. Why are you cooking anyway?"

"Mike has a potluck at work tomorrow and has to bring something from home, enough for the whole office to eat. I don't think I could make enough food for all those men. They could each eat their own pan of lasagna."

I laughed as I backed out of the kitchen. "Goodnight, Mom." I trudged upstairs and got ready for bed, climbed under the covers and called Bryan. When he picked up on the second ring, I couldn't help but smile.

The next morning, I woke up feeling that something was off. Immediately I turned over to see what time it was. The clock was blinking 12:00. I groaned as it dawned on me that we must have lost power in the middle of the night. I jumped out of bed and pulled on a pair of jeans and one of my old camp T-shirts.

As I made my way down the stairs, I looked at my phone to see that it was really 9:05. So far I had only missed the first two periods of school. Not that I was complaining. I hated Calculus, and Physics wasn't my best subject. As I pulled into the school parking lot at 9:30, I was debating whether to wait in my car for the last 30 minutes of my third period Latin class or brace myself and walk in late. Finally, against my better judgment, I climbed out of my car and started walking to the main office. Mrs. Garland didn't even look at me when I walked in. Even when I approached her desk, she kept her head down until I cleared my throat.

"Excuse me, Mrs. Garland." Don't get me wrong, Mrs. Garland wasn't a mean lady. She was in her late 40's and was really nice once you got to have an actual conversation with her. She was a little bit shorter than me, and wobbled a little when she walked. She used to have this calm aura around her whenever you came near her, but ever since her husband filed for divorce, everything about her seemed tense. She used to wear dresses that flowed down her body. But now, like today, she was wearing a tight blouse that she had buttoned all the way to the top, so it almost looked like it was choking her. Along with that, she had on a tight waist skirt that went to her knees. So whenever she tried to walk, she could barely separate her legs. It almost seemed like any minute she was going to fall over. As she finally looked up at me, I saw that she even replaced her contacts with big bulky glasses and instead of taking time to do her hair, she just let it lay flat on her head.

"Miss Carpenter, what can I do for you?" She did her best to give me a smile, but I could see every ounce of effort it took her. It was almost as if it was easier for her to frown these days. Not wanting to waste any of her time, I replied quickly.

"May I have a pass to third period? We lost power during the night and my alarm clock didn't go off this morning." As she started writing out the pass, I asked, "How have you been?" She stopped writing the pass abruptly, right in the middle of signing her signature. She instantly tore off the pass and slammed it on the table. As I reached to pick it up, she quickly pulled it out of my reach.

"Katie, I think I have been more than lenient on your tardiness this year because of everything you have gone through. But this is getting ridiculous. Next time, I will not give you a pass to class. Is that understood?" I nodded as I quickly grabbed the note out of her hand and started to back away toward the door. As I slid through the door, I bumped into someone. Without even looking at who it was I knew, just based on the smell of his cologne. I looked up into Chase's blue eyes.

"Chase? Hey. How have you been? I..." My voice trailed off as I noticed his facial expression change when he saw it was me. His once smiling, apologetic face was now sadness mixed with what looked like regret and disgust. As he looked down at me, he exhaled loudly almost as if to actually show his resentment toward me. He started to walk past me when I stuck my arm in between him and the office door. When he ran into my arm, he looked down at me again and said with a harsh, menacing voice, "What do you want, Katie?"

Then his voice lowered until it was almost as if he was a little boy and he was upset about something that had happened previously. "Will you please just leave me alone?"

He drew in a deep breath when I slowly shook my head.

"You know I won't, Chase. You know me better than that. I want my best friend back."

His voice was raised with anger and annoyance as he responded, "You can't have it both ways, so stop trying. I need you to leave me alone, and I need you to respect that." He started backing away.

I wasn't going to let him get away that easy so I yelled, "You can't keep ignoring me!"

He stopped quickly and turned towards me as he said, "Watch me." And with those two words, he turned around and walked away from me.

CHAPTER 23

I don't know why I didn't go after Chase. I felt like a part of me was missing. I didn't want a relationship with him that is anything more than friends, but how could I be happy when my best friend walks out of my life for good?

As if on cue, my phone rang.

"Bryan?" I smiled as I heard him say my name. "Everything okay?"

"Yeah, everything is fine. I just wanted to let you know that my mom has a doctor's appointment that I have to take her to, so I can't come over. But if you're free tomorrow, I'll be there whenever you tell me to be. Promise."

I smiled. "That's fine. Call me when you get home." When he agreed, I relaxed and my world went back to being normal. "Bye."

As I slid my phone back into my purse, the bell rang that ended third period, so I changed direction and started walking to my fourth period class.

When I walked into class, the first thing I noticed was that the desk next to mine that had always been empty was now occupied. The only thing on the desk was a backpack, so whoever now occupied the seat was nowhere to be seen.

As I looked around the classroom, I saw someone leaning over the teacher's desk. He was wearing purple vans, black shorts and a purple button down shirt.

When I finally looked up at the face of the new guy in class, I froze. Of course, it would be Chase, sitting right next to me, after he had just walked out of my life. As he walked over to the back corner where our desks were, I stared at him still frozen in place. He wouldn't look at me. He just kept looking straight ahead. When he reached his seat, he faced the front of the classroom so there was no way I could make eye contact with him.

When the bell rang for class to start, the remaining kids that weren't in the classroom quickly shuffled in to take their seats. They were trying to avoid the teacher seeing them, so they wouldn't be counted tardy. Of course, she saw every single one of them.

Mrs. McLean turned the lights off and the projector on to start her lecture on Business Management, always a sure bet to make me fall asleep. But as I laid my head down, I found I couldn't sleep.

It felt weird being in close proximity to Chase, yet not talking. I was about to say something, something that I hoped would fix everything. But as I was gathering the words, someone beat me to it. I looked to the right of me to see Natalie, the girl sitting in front of Chase, turn and start whispering.

"So you're new to this class, right?" I wanted to

smack the smirk on her face all the way over to the other side of the classroom, but I decided against it. Then before Chase even had time to answer, she answered her own question with a whispered, "Well, obviously, I mean I think I would have remembered someone like you sitting behind me. Since I don't, I'm going to guess that you're new."

I knew that if I was Chase, I would have had a few words for her, probably starting with the fact that she talked too much. But I knew Chase would never say that. He was too nice for that, clearly nicer than me.

I head Chase chuckle before answering her in his own whisper, "Yeah, I'm new. They dissolved my other business class because my class only had twelve students. So here I am."

Natalie started giggling like he said something funny, when really all he was doing was answering her question. I could almost see Chase's eyes rolling, but I wasn't going to look over at him. I wasn't going to give in first. I thought for sure their conversation was going to be over, but she kept finding new things to talk to him about.

"I'm Natalie, by the way." She held out her hand for him to shake, which he did.

"Chase. I think I met you last year though. Brittany introduced us."

"OMG." You're totally right! I thought I recognized you. Sorry!" Another giggling attack came over her as a sudden urge came over me to slam my head into the wall behind me repeatedly; maybe that would get me away from her desperate attempt to flirt.

"Anyways, you're not like dating anyone are you?" She asked as she annoyingly twirled her hair between her fingers, intertwining the strands. It almost looked like she was trying to tie a big knot with her hair. It took Chase a while to answer. So long in fact, that I was actually about to look over at him to make sure he was okay.

But before I looked at him, he took a deep breath and awkwardly answered. Well, awkward on my part, because of what just went down in the hallway.

"Um, no, I'm not. But I'm not really looking either, so..." I glanced at him out of the corner of my eye and saw him messing with his hands.

I heard a faint noise and noticed that it was Natalie breathing a long sigh before turning around to face the teacher. I very stealthily slid a piece of paper out of my binder and started to write on it.

"Just go out with her, Chase. Get it over with." When I was done writing, I folded it twice so it made a perfect square, leaned over to my right and laid it on his desk; all without taking my eyes off the teacher. Honestly, I was surprised he even opened it and read it. I thought that meant he was going to write back, but instead, he quickly read it and set it back down on the desk. I let out a big sigh. I was frustrated with the fact that my best friend was no longer communicating with me. I was frustrated that the choice that I had to make, which in the end wasn't a choice, was going to hurt someone. But most of all, I was frustrated because I cared way more than I should that Chase walked out of my life. Not the best feeling in the world, by a long shot.

I reached across Chase and grabbed the piece of paper with more force than necessary and slammed it back down on my desk. The sound was loud enough to get everyone in the class to turn around and look at me. To top it off, it got Mrs. McLean to stop her lecture, making it the first time she has EVER stopped a lecture. I put my arms over the note and just smiled.

After taking a few minutes to glare at me, Mrs. McLean turned around and started talking again, almost as if nothing had stopped her in the first place. Weird. When the whole class finally turned their attention back to the teacher, I heard Chase chuckling. I wanted to punch him. Of course that might not turn out so great, so I quickly pushed that thought aside. As I began to write something else, the bell rang. Before I could even look up, Chase was halfway to the door. I could see the window of opportunity to get our relationship back to how it used to be quickly escaping my grasp.

CHAPTER 24

"Dude, that's so gross! Your horse is still pooping even though it's walking!" Sam yelled up to Bryan as Scotty started laughing.

After school that day, Bryan invited me to go on a horseback ride with all the guys from the vineyard. I said no at first, but when Scotty and Sam showed up at my house and practically pulled me away, I reluctantly agreed. As soon as we got to the barn, the twins started complaining about the smell. They still weren't sure why Bryan worked here instead of working at the vineyard. At this point, we were a good three miles into our ride. I was riding behind Bryan with my hands firmly around his waist. I could feel Bryan laughing.

"Sam, you're acting like you have never ridden a horse before. It's normal for them to poop while walking." I turned around in the saddle and sure enough, the horse we were on was still pooping.

I started giggling as I said, "But that really is gross." We rode in silence the remainder of the ride. I wasn't exactly sure where we were going. All I knew was that wherever it was, we were going to have a picnic. We came up on a hill that overlooked a pond. On the edge of the pond, there was a pier that you could use for fishing. I looked around and noticed that on the side of Greg's horse, he had four fishing poles. I quickly got off the horse and walked over to the edge of the water. "So what first, eating or fishing?"

Scotty popped out from behind his horse and said, "Fishing, duh!" I looked over at him and noticed that he had half a sandwich in his hand. After a few minutes, all of us had cast out into the water. Bryan had volunteered to share a fishing pole with someone, and then I volunteered to share with him. None of the guys were surprised that we were the ones sharing. Scotty looked over at me. "So, Katie, have you given any thought to your big plans after high school?"

I shook my head as I looked over at him. "I haven't even thought about it. I heard it's better to live in the moment." I smiled over at Bryan.

Keeping his attention on his fishing line, Sam said, "Yeah, that's great until your moment becomes graduation and you haven't planned anything after that, so you end up working at a vineyard."

"But then you can't see yourself doing anything but working at the vineyard, because everyone there is like a family," Scotty added.

I was kind of surprised that this was the twins talking. The same twins that couldn't go five minutes without making fun of something or someone.

I looked over at Bryan. "What are your plans?" He glanced at me, then cleared his throat.

"Work at the vineyard. It's growing pretty fast and your dad offered me a permanent job, but only if I take classes at the community college." I nodded. My dad mentioned that he was going to offer Bryan a job. With the events of the past couple of years, I hadn't really given any thought to my future. Because if the past years have taught me anything, it's that I have to live in the moment because nobody is guaranteed the next one.

The next day, I was walking to Business Management, dreading the moment I would see Chase. He had been cleverly avoiding me all day, but I wasn't surprised. I had lost him. Somewhere deep down inside, I always knew that if I stayed with Bryan, Chase was going to get hurt. Time after time, Chase always forgave me, but I guess some things have to end. I had finally pushed him over his breaking point, and I didn't do anything to prevent him from falling.

I knew one thing was true now. If you keep pushing someone away, one day they won't return. But then what do you do? After all the pushing is done and your lives become separate, then what? How was I supposed to let my best friend just walk away like that after everything we've been through?

When I walked into class, I expected to see Chase begging for a seat change, but he was sitting in the corner desk in the back of the classroom right next to me like yesterday. When I went to sit down, I couldn't help but notice his outfit, baby blue vans, khaki pants, and a baby blue v-neck shirt. Classic Chase. I quickly took my seat as the bell rang, avoiding his eyes. I was staring at the clock when all of a sudden, I heard Mrs.

McLean start talking about a partner project that we would be starting, so I began to pay attention.

"The point of this project is to create a business and explain what that business will do. You will need to choose where it will be located and do research about that city and explain why you chose that location. There will be an essay at the end about your research. Then you must create an action plan about building your business and make a computerized scale model of your building. The last detail of your project will be to create positions and write about how they will help make your business successful. The completed project should either be in a PowerPoint or on a poster. I will be assigning your partner." She picked up a piece of paper on her desk and started reading off names.

"Rebecca and Sarah, Austin and Amy, Luke and Ryan, Michelle and Courtney…" There were a few high fives going around and squeals from Michelle and Courtney when they heard that they were going to be partners. "Travis and Brianna, Megan and Jeremy, Fredy and Brenda, Chase and Katie…" My head shot up and I looked at her. She couldn't have just said that. The one person I didn't want to be with, I was partnered with. I would rather be with snotty Sam, or Michelle who wore way to much perfume. I got up and headed to the computer we would be working with for the re-mainder of the project. I looked around for Chase and spotted him talking to Mrs. McLean. I could only make out a few words that Chase was saying; "…mistake…

can't work with…new partners." I looked over at Mrs. McLean to see what she would say. She just shook her head and said, "Get started…" He sighed and trudged over to the computer I was at and swiftly rolled a chair next to me.

I quietly said under my breath, "Denied…" I looked at him through the corner of my eye and he was staring at me like I had just committed a federal offense. "What?"

"Nothing," he muttered quietly and logged on to the computer. He reached over me so he could use the mouse. Instinctively, I pulled the mouse out of his reach and he looked at me. "Do you have a problem?"

I shook my head as I replied, "No, do you?"

"Look, can we just work on this? I don't want to be your partner any more than you want to be mine. So let's get this over with. Okay?"

"That's just it, Chase, I want to be your partner." Chase lightly cleared his throat as he stood up and went over to the door, grabbed the hall pass and walked out of the room. I sighed and without thinking, got out of my seat and walked out of class. Chase had barely made it to the next classroom door before I caught up to him. "Wait, what are you doing?"

"What am I doing? What are *you* doing? Every time we have a conversation, every single time, you say something like that."

"Like what?" I honestly didn't know what he was referring to. "Chase, I—"

"You say stuff like 'I want to be your partner' or 'I miss you'—"

"It's because I—"

He put his hand up. "Let me talk!" He clasped his hands together in a motion that looked like he was about to pray. "You say all that stuff, then you leave here and say the exact same stuff to Bryan. You chose him. I didn't get a choice in this and yet, I'm the one suffering the most and it doesn't help that you prance around telling me that you miss me. I know you miss me, I get it. But it doesn't make this any less painful for me! I'm tired of coming up second. I deserve someone who wants me and nobody else. But I can't even begin to move on if you don't let me!" Before I could say anything in response, I heard heels clacking on the floor behind us.

"Chase, if you don't need to go to the restroom, I suggest you get inside. Katie, if you leave my class like that again, there will be consequences. Do I make myself clear?" We both nodded and walked back inside the classroom. We could tell that the class had heard everything Mrs. McCleary had just said because there was a lot of whispering going on.

When we sat down, there were a couple minutes of awkward silence between Chase and I until I asked, "So what do you want our business to be?"

"I don't know."

"Okay. Where do you want it to be located?"

"I don't care."

I sighed loudly and sat back in my chair in defeat. If he wasn't going to give me any ideas, then I don't know how we are supposed to do this at all. It was impossible. I truly believed that we weren't going to get anything done on this project. I cleared my throat and whispered quietly to show him that I wasn't going to lose my temper.

"Fine, how about we just don't do anything and we can fail it?"

"How about we do a restaurant? It's simple, it's easy." He wouldn't look at me as he spoke, he just stared at the computer screen. I nodded and handed him the mouse. He gently took it and gave me a weak smile.

Two weeks later, it seemed like everything was getting back to the way they used to be. Chase came over to work on the project whenever I wasn't spending time with Bryan. The project was going amazingly well. We almost had it complete. The floor plan, the positions, what we would serve, where it's located. We just had to put everything on a poster board, which we waited until the last night to do. I reached past him to grab the scissors to start cutting out pictures of our food items.

"Do you want the floor plan to be in the corner or the center of the poster board?" He turned towards me as he asked that.

"The center for sure," I responded. "I still can't believe we're matching." I looked up at him. He was wearing a black New York Yankees hat perched on the top of his head and a white v-neck shirt with black basketball shorts, black socks, and black slides on his feet. I was wearing a white "Save the Trees" shirt, black Nike shorts and black flip flops.

"If we opened this restaurant someday, it would kick butt. The best food, best service, best uniform…"

"Don't forget the two hot owners!" We laughed in unison. Things between Chase and I had lightened up and it wasn't as tense as before. I was about to talk about our presentation that we had to make the following day when the doorbell rang. As I walked closer to the door, I wondered who it could be. Mike and my mom were out of town for their anniversary, and I wasn't expecting anyone. When I opened the door and looked up at Bryan, I froze. I walked outside on the porch and closed the door behind me.

"Hey, babe." Bryan's smile gleamed under the porch light.

"What are you doing here?"

Bryan looked at me with a puzzled expression on his face. "You told me last week that Mike was taking your mom to some resort that was out of town, and told me to come over for some movies. I even brought pizza." He held up the pizza box.

"I totally forgot. I'm actually working on a project tonight, so it's not really a good time. Why don't I just come over tomorrow?"

"Well, how about I help you on your project while

we eat this pizza?" He gave me his half smile and I just sighed and walked into the house. When I walked in, Chase was standing by the bottom of the stairs.

"What's going on out there?" Chase was smiling, but it quickly faded when Bryan walked in behind me. "Oh, I see. Well, I better get going."

I held my hand out in front of him. "Chase, wait! We need to finish this project. Bryan can help."

Chase snorted, "Yeah, right! I don't need help from him. I can take the project home and finish it for us."

I was about to say something when I heard Bryan's voice behind me. "Dude, get over yourself. I'm not here to do anything but spend time with my girlfriend. Alright?"

I closed my eyes when Bryan said girlfriend. It wasn't necessary for him to throw that word in there. My friendship with Chase was delicate enough and Bryan saying girlfriend didn't help. I was hoping Chase wouldn't pick up on that or at least say anything, but of course he did.

"Smooth. Let's just throw in the fact that she's your girlfriend, like I didn't already know." Chase walked back over to the kitchen table and started picking up the poster board. I ran over to him and put my hand on his shoulder.

"Please just stay so we can finish this, then you never have to see him again. I promise."

"Katie, I—" he sighed as he looked up at me. "Fine."

I nodded. "Okay then. I'm going to go get some more

scissors from the study." I looked from Chase to Bryan, then back to Chase. "Play nice." I smiled as I walked over to the study which was towards the front of the house. I looked in the top drawer of the desk for the scissors, but couldn't find them. So I started looking through the rest of the desk drawers hunting for scissors.

That's when I heard Bryan's raised voice asking, "What do you have against me?"

"Dude, if you really don't know, then you're dumber than I thought." Chase yelled back.

"Don't get an attitude with me. I'm not trying to be your friend."

"Then why are you talking to me?" Chase almost yelled, which made me go through all the drawers a lot faster so I could get back in the kitchen before something happened between them. I heard muffled voices and then something fell to the floor with a crash. I ran into the kitchen and saw a lamp shattered on the floor. Beside it, Chase was on the ground with blood dripping from the corner of his mouth onto his white shirt. A piece of glass shaped like a triangle stuck in his hand. I stood at the bottom of the stairs in disbelief as I looked at Bryan.

"What the——?" I shook my head while Bryan said, "Katie, I'm sorry, but I just stuck my hand out to make him stop talking."

"Stop, Bryan, just stop. Feel free to wait in my room until Chase leaves. I'll be up whenever I can." He nodded as he walked past me and up the stairs.

CHAPTER 25

As I started to dab Chase's busted lip with a wet cloth, he winced in pain.

"Sorry." I said as I dipped the cloth back into the bowl of warm water.

Chase gently grabbed my hand as he moved over on the couch to make room for me.

"You can sit next to me, I won't bite." He joked, as a smirk appeared on his lips and he winced from the pain. "I can clean my own face, you know?"

"No, I can do it. It's my fault anyway. I—"

"This isn't your fault, Katie. Bryan punched me and I fell into the lamp. You didn't do anything. Promise." He gave a weak smile that didn't cause him pain as I began dabbing his chin, now covered with blood.

"Chase, can I ask you something?"

"Sure."

I smiled at his response as I asked, "Why did Bryan punch you?"

Chase took in a deep exaggerated breath. "It happened so quickly, but I might have said something that provoked it—"

"What did you say?" I questioned.

"Something along the lines of…you deserve better. But I didn't mean it like I was better. I just meant in general, someone like Lucas." My head shot up when he said Lucas's name, and I started to gently shake my head.

"Nobody will ever be like Lucas, but Bryan is right for me. Even if Lucas was still here, Bryan would have still been the one."

Chase stood up quickly. "No! You don't know that. I—"

He sat back down next to me. "I'm trying not to yell anymore. I think we have done enough of that for a while." He chuckled and then his face grew serious. "I'm glad you're in my life again. It feels good."

I smiled and put the blood-stained cloth in the bowl. "Well, you're all cleaned up. I can finish the project if you want to head home."

Chase laughed and said, "I think you have enough on your hands tonight." He pointed to the stairs. "I can finish it." Then he walked over to the kitchen table and grabbed the poster and all the charts. As we walked out of the kitchen, neither of us spoke. He broke the silence when we got to the door. "Well, thanks for the interesting evening." He smiled, then reached up and moved a strand of hair out of my face and put it behind my ear. "Goodnight, Katie." He started to walk down the steps, then turned around and whispered, "Good luck." I smiled as I whispered back "Goodnight" and closed the door.

I stopped at the foot of the stairs and just looked up. I sighed and went over to the couch where the bowl of blood-stained water sat. I picked it up and went into the kitchen to dump the water in the sink. I grabbed a green sponge and some antibacterial soap and started scrubbing the bowl. When the bowl was clean, I squeezed the water out of the sponge before storing it under the sink.

When there was nothing left for me to clean up, I looked over at the clock. It was 11:45. It had only been 30 minutes since Chase left. I hesitantly walked up the stairs, not in the mood to get into a fight with Bryan. When I walked into my room, I saw him sitting in the wooden antique chair that sat in the corner of my room. The old rocking chair used to be in that spot. He was looking out of the window, but turned toward me when I walked into the room. I walked over to my bed and sat down in the center of it, crossed my legs and stared down at my hands resting in my lap. After a few minutes of silence, Bryan cleared his throat, and moved uncomfortably in the chair. I looked at him from the corner of my eye, and then looked away.

Finally, he broke the silence. "The silent treatment. Really, Katie? Are we in kindergarten again?"

"I guess so, because what you did tonight was something a child would do." I glared at him.

"I said I was sorry, and I am. I just got defensive and thought I was protecting you somehow. Things just got out of hand." He gently stood up and came to sit on the corner of my bed. When he did, I stood up and went to lean against the wall beside my closet. He sighed. "How long is this going to go on? There isn't anything I can do now, so why can't we just move on?"

"Move on? You punched my best friend!" I didn't realize I was shouting until he stood up with a surprised look on his face.

"Did you just say best friend? Katie, you only started talking to him again two weeks ago! For the first week you couldn't stand the guy, now all of a sudden he's your best friend after all that time of ignoring each other?"

"Time doesn't change how I feel."

"Well, if time doesn't change how you feel, then do you still care about him?"

"He's my best friend!"

Bryan put his hands up as if a cop had just caught him red handed. "It was just a simple question."

"Well, I gave you a simple answer."

Bryan walked over to me and put his hands up against the wall on both sides of my head and whispered, "I hate this. I hate fighting with you. I'm sorry for what I did. But I will always put you first, no matter what. I will always protect you, I promise."

I shook my head and as I pushed against his chest, I whispered, "Don't make promises you can't keep." I walked over to the dresser and grabbed a pair of grey sweatpants and a three-quarter length baseball tee and brushed past him as I went into the bathroom to change.

When I got to the bathroom, I stared at myself in the mirror for a few seconds before slipping off my shirt and jeans, and replacing them with my sweat-pants and shirt. After brushing my teeth and washing my face, I returned to my room to find Bryan sitting on my bed with his hands in his lap and his head down. I saw he was wearing black Sperry's with faded blue jeans and a white v-neck shirt. His black leather jacket was draped over the chair.

I walked over and sat down next to him. I sighed, reached over and grabbed one of his hands. As I in-tertwined our fingers together, his body relaxed. He looked over at me and gave me a faint smile.

"I'm going to keep my promise to you, Katie. You are the most important thing in my life. I love you, and I am so sorry about tonight, about everything." When his voice started shaking, I could see the rims of his eyes were turning red. "I never meant to hurt you."

"I just don't understand. The Bryan I know would never punch anybody."

"I don't know what got into me, but that guy wasn't me." He sighed. "There's something I need to tell you." He pulled his hand away from mine and cov-ered his face with his hands. "It's my mom. I think she's drinking again. I've been trying to help her, but I can't. She won't listen because she doesn't think anything is wrong."

I pulled his hands away from his face and held them in mine. "Bryan, I think you need to send her to that rehab place in Texas. They have the best ratings. They can help her turn her life around."

He shook his head. "I can't send her away. She's all I have. Without her, I'll be alone." He looked away from me and just stared at the wall.

I placed my hand gently on the side of his face pointed away from me and moved his head until he was looking me in the eyes. "You will have me." I smiled as he leaned over and kissed me.

He shrugged as he said, "I just can't send her away."

I leaned over and kissed his cheek before saying, "Promise me something." Bryan nodded lightly. "Promise you won't leave me."

He smiled and said "Promise." He leaned over and kissed me gently. I smiled and crawled over to the top of the bed and got under the covers. Bryan stood up. "I guess that's your way of kicking me out." He chuckled. "Goodnight, Katie."

When he got to the door I said, "You promised." He turned to face me with a half-smile on his lips.

"I didn't know you meant tonight." He walked over to my bed, slipping off his shoes and climbed under the covers. He pulled me close to him and I rested my head on his chest.

Before I knew it, my alarm was blaring and it was 6:30 in the morning. I groaned as I rolled over and turned it off. I looked over at Bryan, who was rubbing his eyes.

"Good morning."

He chuckled, then pulled me towards him and kissed my forehead. "Good morning." I pulled away and got out of bed. I stumbled towards my closet before pulling out a pair of faded skinny jeans and a purple crew cut shirt.

"You mind if I shower?"

His voice took me by surprise because I was still half asleep. "Of course not, go ahead. I'll show you where everything is." I led him out my door and to the right. My bathroom was filled with blue and white striped wallpaper, and had a silver theme...silver handles on the cabinets and drawers, silver soap container, silver Kleenex holder, silver toothbrush holder, silver rack to hold the bath towels. I went over to the shower and turned it on. "So hot is this way" and I pointed to the right. "Cold is the other way." I walked over to the cabinet under the sink and pulled out a towel. "You can just use my shampoo and soap. Other than that, that's pretty much it. I have to leave for school in twenty minutes, so don't take an hour-long shower." He chuckled and nodded.

I closed the door that separated the shower and the toilet, so I could still use the sink and mirror. After changing into my jeans and crew shirt, I pulled my bangs out of my face using a brown bobby pin. Then I reached into my drawer and pulled out my contact case. After unscrewing the top, I placed the contacts in my eyes. After brushing my teeth, I heard the water turn off in the bathroom, so I walked back to my room to give him some privacy. I was slipping on a denim jacket when he sauntered into my room, slipping on his shirt as he walked. I chuckled.

"What?" He smiled.

"You really couldn't put your shirt on in the bathroom?"

"You said to hurry, so I thought it would be faster if I came in here and put it on. Anyway, I've got to get going. I have an hour to drive and I'm going to be late to class as it is." He walked over and kissed me, "I love you."

I smiled up at him, "Love you, too. Text me when you get to school."

He nodded as he responded, "Will do." Then he was gone.

When I walked into Business Management, I was greeted by a warm hug from Chase. I looked up at his lip to see the beginnings of a scab that ran from the inside part of his lip to the outside. He saw me looking at it and reached up to touch it, wincing as he did.

I quickly asked, "How does it feel?"

"It hurts." He looked around the room before walking me to our corner. After we both sat down, he turned in his desk and said, "How bad did you yell at Bryan?"

I hesitated before answering. "I walked up there planning to kill him, but couldn't once I saw him."

Chase sighed. "Figures…"

"He said he was sorry."

Chase shrugged, "He's only sorry because he delivered a good punch that made me fall into the lamp, so technically he won."

The school day went by fast. When my parents got home at seven o'clock. I already had fettuccine ready for dinner. As we sat down to eat it, my mom caught me off guard when she asked, "Where's the lamp?" She was looking over by the couch where the lamp usually sat.

"I accidentally ran into it. I'll buy another one. Sorry, Mom."

"Don't be, I always hated that lamp. It's about time it broke." I laughed. When we finished eating and cleaning up the kitchen, it was nine o'clock.

"Well, I'm tired. Long day. I'm going to bed. Goodnight."

When I climbed into bed after my shower, it was ten o'clock. Just as I was dozing off, my phone started ringing. I groaned as I reached over to pick it up.

"Hello?"

"Katie, I need your help. It's my mom." Bryan's panicked voice frightened me. I had never heard him like this. He was breathing heavily on the other end of the line.

"Bryan, what happened?"

"I went straight from your house to school, then from school to work, and I'm just now getting home. My mom's gone. The back door was open, beer bottles everywhere. I have to find her. Please help me."

"Okay, I'll call the cops—"

"No! Whatever you do, don't call the cops. Katie, she's in bad shape. They'll send her to Texas for rehab.

Just promise me you won't," Bryan pleaded.

"Fine, I'll be over at your house in 45 minutes. I'm going to get us more help first."

"I'm going to start checking on the North side of town. As you're coming in from the South, start looking there." Then the line disconnected. I climbed out of bed in a daze and pulled on a sweatshirt. I quietly tiptoed down the stairs and glanced over at my mom and Mike sleeping on the couch. I did my best not to wake them as I opened the front door. As I made my way to my car, I was trying to think of someone I could call to help Bryan and me. Only one name came into my head.

CHAPTER 26

I was about to knock on Chase's door when I realized it might be better to call him. I quickly got out my phone and dialed his number.

"Hello?" Chase's voice was groggy and quiet.

"I need your help, please."

He asked, "Are you okay?" I could hear him shuffling around, probably for a shirt.

"Yeah, I'm fine. I just…just come out here, please." Within a couple minutes, Chase was out of his house. By that time, I had already climbed back into my car. He slowly climbed into the passenger side and closed the door. "We have to go somewhere." Chase looked at me with a confused gaze.

"Okay…You mind telling me where?"

I shook my head. "You trust me, right?

"Yes." He nodded.

"And you want to help me?"

He nodded again slowly.

"Good," I said as I locked the doors and sped out of his driveway. After about ten minutes of silence, the curiosity overcame Chase.

"What exactly am I helping you with?"

"Bryan's mom——"

"Bryan! You're bringing me to help Bryan? The guy who punched me? The guy who has made my life nothing more than a living hell? Please tell me you're not taking me to help *that* Bryan."

I looked at him from the corner of my eye. "Yes. But——"

"I don't believe you! You tricked me! There is no way I'm helping him. No way!"

It suddenly dawned on me that I was putting everything on the line to help Bryan. My relationship with Chase was still on rocky ground. I was just beginning to earn back his trust and this moment could break that trust forever.

"His mom is gone! And he doesn't know where she is! She has a drinking problem and is probably wandering around town drunk! Do you have any idea how dangerous that is? Forget the fact that it's Bryan's mom. Think of her as just a mom in general. She's hurting. What kind of sick person wouldn't help her out?" I expected him to yell back or to make some smart comeback, but instead, he quietly responded. "Okay, I'll help you find her. But I'm not doing it for Bryan." After a couple of minutes in silence, I finally had to speak.

"Look Chase, thank y——"

"You don't have to say anything else about it, I'm helping." I looked over at him and he was staring out the open window, his black hair blowing in the night breeze. I couldn't see the expression on his face since it was almost 11:30. Only when we crossed into town did I dare say another word.

"Keep your eyes open, we're in town."

Chase sighed heavily, "Yeah, why on earth would I want to close my eyes when I'm tired, and its way past the time I usually go to bed." I just rolled my eyes and pulled into a gas station. "What are you doing?"

"It's a small town, Chase. It's easier to look for her if we go on foot." We both climbed out of the car. I looked down the deserted street. The town was small enough that the downtown area consisted of three streets. We started walking toward the part of downtown that had the least amount of buildings in it, just an old house and old farm equipment around it. The old house scared me; its shutters were hanging on by a string of wire wrapped around them. The door was halfway off the hinges. The wood that the house was made out of was rotting and falling apart. I wanted to walk past it, but Chase insisted that we go inside. Once we got close enough to the house, we saw that spider webs covered most of the stairway leading up to the house, and all across the porch was sand and dust.

We walked up the steps. As we put our weight on each solitary step, the whole house seemed to moan. When Chase turned the door handle to open the door, the handle fell to the ground. I would have laughed if I wasn't freaked out about the house. Chase ended up having to run his shoulder into the door, which fell off its hinges onto the dusty wood floor inside the house. I stepped through the doorway and saw that the furniture inside the house was covered with white sheets and dust. The wood floor had cracks and holes in it. The floor was literally rotting under my feet; I could almost feel it. The first room I walked into looked like it was a study at some point. I ran my finger along the bookshelf that was still full of books. They were old books, leather bound and now covered in dust. I pulled one out and blew the dust off the covers. It was a *Tale of Two Cities*. I slid the book gently back onto the shelf. I stepped back slowly, creating distance between the shelf and me before hearing a crack. I lifted my foot up and saw an old picture frame. I picked it up gently and saw that the picture inside the frame was an old black and white picture from a Polaroid camera. It was a middle aged man next to what appeared to be his wife. They were each holding the hand of a little girl who had a big smile on her face. Both of her front teeth were missing.

Chase walked into the study. "Hey, I checked the rest of the house. Nobody's here. It doesn't look like anyone's been here in a while." I was still staring at the picture when he walked over to me. "What are you looking at?" He took the picture from my hands.

"What happened to this house? Nobody would leave that picture frame behind. They looked happy."

"Well, whatever happened, wasn't good. I found bullet holes in the wall upstairs, a lot of them. So their life couldn't have been perfect…" He set the picture down on the desk and asked, "You ready to go?"

"Why couldn't their life be perfect? It's possible."

"Nobody's life is as perfect as they make it seem." He shook his head.

"It could be. Is this about what happened between us?"

Chase chuckled, "What? Not everything is about what happened between us! It doesn't even matter."

"We've never talked about it out in the open. If it would help, maybe we should talk through it," I suggested.

"Why? It wouldn't change anything. There's no point."

Chase turned to leave when I shouted, "You can't avoid that subject forever. Sooner or later, we're going to have to talk about it."

Chase looked at the ground in front of him, his back still towards me, "Katie, leave it alone!" He started to walk out of the room.

"Just talk to me about it." As I was saying this, I reached out and grabbed his arm. Before I knew it, I was slammed into a wall. Chase's hand tightly gripped my elbow, while his other hand gently rested on my waist.

"You want to know how I felt! Abandoned. One moment you were laughing in my arms, then I blinked, and you were in Bryan's. I've been abandoned before. My dad went AWOL, so I get it. But you, I thought you were the one person that would never leave; the one constant in my life. I fought as hard as I could to get you, then I had to fight even harder to keep you.

But it wasn't enough. So there is nothing to talk about. I don't need to talk about it, and I don't need you to keep bringing it up. We're friends again. Can't we just leave it at that?"

Then just like that, I was standing in the creaking house alone. As I left the house, I saw Chase leaning against an old, worn down wooden fence looking out into an open field. We stood in silence for a few minutes. The night had closed in around us, so we could barely see the field. The only light we had was the glow of the full moon, and the stars surrounding it.

I took a deep breath before saying, "Still friends?"

"Of course." Chase didn't look at me, but he wasn't looking at the field anymore. He was looking down at his hands that were folded on top of the fence.

"I'm sorry for making you mad."

Chase finally looked at me with his goofy half smile on his face. "Katie, the one I loved. There are going to be times when we fight, when I get pissed and leave. But that doesn't change the fact that you're my best friend. That in there," he motioned towards the house, "just happened to be one of the times that I got pissed." He chuckled lightly before saying, "Well, enough chit chat, you ready to go look?" While he was over the fence in a single jump, I climbed over slowly, watching where I was putting my feet. When I hit the ground, Chase was standing next to an old tire. For dramatic effect, he was looking at his right wrist, like he was looking at a watch that he didn't have. As I walked over to him, I looked as far into the field as I could see. The only thing visible was a line of trees surrounding the field. I couldn't see that far out in front of me either. As Chase and I walked farther into the field, I became more and more nervous. Not only because we were in an abandoned area of town, but because I couldn't see clearly. Then all of a sudden, I slipped on something and right before I hit the ground, Chase's arm was on my elbow catching me. He chuckled as he said, "Do you know how to walk?" I pushed him away before bending down to find what I had tripped on. It was a glass bottle. There was no label on it, but it was clearly a beer bottle.

"Chase, she's been here." I held up the bottle to him.

"The bottle means nothing, it could be months old." As he said this, I tipped the bottle over and a few drops of fresh beer fell out of it.

"It still has the strong smell of alcohol and there are still drops of it in here. If the bottle had been out here for months, then the smell and the left over drops would be gone."

Chase shrugged. "So some kid comes out here to drink. It's not a bad idea, it's not like people ever come out here."

"I have a feeling she's been here." I shrugged, defeated and not in the mood to argue with him anymore.

He gently pulled me to his chest. "Even if it's hers, she could be anywhere."

We continued to walk around in the big field before something caught my eye. It was a little hole in the woods. I quickly tapped Chase on the shoulder and pointed to it. I whispered gently, "It looks like a trail…" I grabbed Chase's hand and pulled him to the start of the trail. From what I could tell, it was a very rocky, hilly trail. I could only tell that based on the shadows of the boulders and trees because there was no light other than the glow of the moon. I took a step forward, but Chase pulled me back.

"No, Katie, at least wait until morning. You could get lost."

"If Bryan's mom is in there, she needs me. I'm going in, feel free to join me." I pulled my hand out of Chase's and started walking down the trail. A few seconds later, I heard Chase jog in after me. After a few minutes of walking blindly down the trail, I heard moaning. I started to walk a little faster when I saw her. She was lying down against a tree, a beer bottle in one hand. "Chase, can you carry her?" Before I could even finish the sentence, Chase was already sliding his hands under her knees and behind her back. Julie was mumbling something, but I couldn't make out what she was saying. I pulled out my phone to call Bryan, but as I dialed his number, my phone beeped. "Darn it…no signal."

"Let's just get out of here. We can call Bryan later." After Chase said this, he walked past me back the way we had come. We walked in silence until we got to the open field. Chase said, "She's out cold…" I didn't say anything. I just kept walking. My phone beeped letting me know that I had signal. I dialed Bryan's number again. When he picked up, he was out of breath.

"Hey, Katie, please tell me you found her…"

"We did. She's okay."

Bryan heaved a sigh of relief. "Oh thank God. Can I talk to her?"

"She's out cold. We don't know how many beers she had. We're headed back to your house, meet you there."

As I broke the connection, Chase whispered, "Katie, we have a problem." I turned to face him and saw his hands were stained red. "She hit her head."

When we pulled into Bryan's driveway, it was 5:30. Before Chase could come to a complete stop, Bryan had the back door open. I reached behind me and put my hand on his mom's shoulder.

"Bryan, don't move her. We have an ambulance on the way. She hit her head pretty badly on something."

Bryan backed up, and his face went hard as he put his hands behind his head. He wouldn't look me in the eye as he said, "I need a minute." He walked into the house and shut the door. I sighed and looked over at Chase who was staring at his jacket, now under Julie's head soaking up the blood. A few minutes later, the ambulance stopped in front of Bryan's house. From then on, everything seemed to move fast. Chase and I were asked a lot of questions about everything that happened. Bryan came out of the house to help put his mom in the ambulance. I could tell he was a wreck. After I finished giving my statement, I turned around to see if Bryan was still outside, but he wasn't. One of the cops said he rode in the ambulance to the hospital.

I walked over to Chase. "Hey, I'm going to go to the hospital to check up on everyone. Are you coming?"

Chase chuckled, "I guess. You are my ride home, you know?"

CHAPTER 27

When we got to the small country hospital, we walked into the ER. I saw a red-headed nurse on the phone. She looked like she was in her 40's. When she hung up the phone, she looked at me and smiled.

"Can I help you?"

"Yes, I'm looking for——" and then I saw Bryan walk out of a room, so I looked back at the nurse. "Never mind." Then I walked to Julie's room. I saw the twins and Greg. I smiled as I walked over and gave them all a hug. "What are y'all doing here?"

Scotty jumped up to receive my hug and gave me a tight squeeze. "Hey, kid! It's about time you showed up." When Chase walked in the room, Scotty stepped back to look at him. "You must be the hero?" He chuckled as he put his hand out for Chase to shake. "I'm Scotty, and that's Sam and Greg."

Chase smiled as he shook hands with Scotty. "I wouldn't say hero, but I was there when we found her."

Sam stood up as he said, "Like Scotty said, you're a hero."

Chase shrugged. "How do you all know each other?" He pointed between the three guys and me.

Greg smiled, "We work at the vineyard." Chase raised his eyebrows and gave him a confused expression, so Greg said, "Her dad's vineyard?"

Chase exhaled. "Oh, right." He chuckled, "I guess I didn't realize how much it's grown. How many acres is it?"

Scotty scoffed lightly. "Over one hundred acres of long, hard work every freaking day."

"Are you complaining about having a job?" I glared at him, but couldn't hold a straight face for long.

Sam threw his arm around Scotty. "What he means is over one hundred acres of love and devotion."

Chase smiled. "Nice save. So it's just the four of you that work there?"

"No, there are five of us, but boss man says we're expanding in acres and in workers," Greg said before shrugging.

I interrupted this male bonding time by asking, "How is Julie doing?" I pointed to the woman who was still lying there unconscious while the boys talked about jobs and raises.

Greg looked over at Julie. "Doc said she has a concussion and lost a lot of blood, but she's going to be fine."

"And Bryan?"

"He's going a little crazy. I think this just hasn't sunk in yet. So Chase, do you play any sports?" Scotty answered.

I rolled my eyes as the boys started talking about stuff that really mattered, like sports. I walked out of the room and saw Bryan standing outside the hospital.

He was leaning against the wall. I stepped outside next to him.

He looked over at me and pulled me to his chest. "Thanks for finding her."

I took a deep breath before saying, "Bryan, I think it's time to send her to rehab. After tonight…I mean, it could have been a lot worse. We're lucky she didn't bleed to death. Besides, Texas isn't that far…" I trailed off when he looked away towards the single highway that ran through the town.

After a few seconds of sitting in silence he whispered, "You're right, I can't help her." He looked down at the ground as his hands now rested in his pockets. "I just had a hard time admitting it because I knew it was my fault that my dad drove off the bridge. I just thought that if I could help my mom, if I could save her, then it would cancel out what happened to my dad. But her problem is too big for me."

"I know how you feel." Bryan and I both jumped at the sound of Chase's voice. He was leaning against the doorframe of the back door. He slowly started walking towards us. "My dad and I didn't get along, even when I was little. When I was five, I was a smart ass. We couldn't agree on anything. We would fight over what baseball game to watch, or where we wanted to go for dinner. But my mom always took my side because I was just a kid, even though that was screwing up her marriage. I was more important. The fights between my dad and I became fights between him and my mom.

So by the time I was seven, my dad just didn't come home one day. I know it's my fault he left. He couldn't handle the fighting anymore. Bryan, I get it. I know what it feels like, the feeling that you screwed up your family. You just have to let go of the pain and regret." Chase was now standing right in front of Bryan, who had placed his full and undivided attention on Chase.

"Thank you, for everything." Bryan held out his hand for Chase to shake.

Chase smiled as he grabbed Bryan's hand. "No problem. I hope everything with your mom works out." Chase hugged me lightly before heading back to my car and climbed in the front seat.

I looked back at Bryan and pointed back to my car. "Well, I should probably get him home. It's about seven and we have school soon."

"You should get yourself home, too. I think I'm going to stay up here all day."

I nodded as I leaned forward and kissed him. "I love you, Bryan."

Bryan smiled at me. "And I love you." I turned around and walked to my car.

When I got in, Chase said, "Next time you want my help, make sure I know how long it's going to take."

I smiled as I punched him lightly. "Wasn't it worth it? We found her, and I think you just gained a friend."

Chase chuckled. "Since when does understanding mean friendship?"

I glanced over at him before starting my car. "You'd

be surprised how much in common the two of you have." Chase shook his head and before he could make another snarky comment, I added, "I don't think I'm going to school today actually. Do you want me to drop you off still?"

Chase shook his head. "Then I guess I won't either. Just drop me off at my house." We drove in silence the rest of the way to his house. The sun was starting to come up over the horizon. Watching a sunset always gives me the feeling that a new day is coming and everything is about to get better. The sky was turning pink and orange as the sun peaked above all of the houses. When I pulled into Chase's house, his mom was already gone for work. He got out of the car, but stood there for a second before asking, "You want to come inside?"

I looked at him and nodded, "Sure." I turned my car off before following him inside the house. I remember when I used to come to his house every day after school because his mom was never home. We climbed the stairs to go to his room where I immediately crawled into his queen size bed. I leaned against two of his pillows as he grabbed one of his Xbox 360 controllers. Chase put in Modern Warfare 3, before sitting down beside me on the bed. He turned the console on before signing onto Xbox Live. He started playing Team Death match with random people, before I cleared my throat.

He glanced over at me and smiled. "What?"

"Oh, nothing. It's not like I didn't want to play or anything!" I punched him lightly.

"Hey!" When I punched him again, he pushed me down on his bed and restrained my hands with his hands as he leaned over me, "Can you calm down?" When I nodded, he let me go before we both sat back up laughing. He picked up his controller and started playing again.

I scoffed before saying, "Chase!"

He looked over at me. "Katie, just let me finish this death match, then we can play. Okay?" He smiled over at me. When I gave him my puppy dog face, he groaned as he turned off the console. "I hate that face. Well, no, I don't, it's just…" He shook his head and didn't bother finishing his sentence. He quickly handed me a controller before getting back to the main screen of the game. After an hour of playing Call of Duty, I was bored. I put my controller back on his dresser. When he started to play another round of Xbox live, I laid down on his bed to watch him. But within minutes, I was fast asleep.

A few hours later I woke up to Chase tapping me on the leg.

I groaned. "What?" I looked up at him.

"You can stay here and sleep, but I actually have plans tonight." I raised my eyebrows. His hair was damp, which means he had just taken a shower. A black flat bill New York Yankees hat rested on his head. He was wearing faded jeans with a fitted plain blue shirt and a black leather jacket. He slid his hands into his jacket pockets.

"Are you going on a date? You should have told me, I could have left earlier." I started to climb out of his bed and quickly scrambled to get my shoes, when I felt his hand rest on my shoulder.

"Katie, calm down. I'm not going on a date." I looked over at him without saying anything. A few seconds later, he shrugged, "Bryan and I are going to the Yankees game tonight. He didn't tell you?"

I shook my head. Why wouldn't Bryan tell me that? "Why are y'all going?"

"He texted me this morning, thanking me again. We figured if we both want to keep you in our lives, then we should try to be friends. So I asked him to go to this game with me." He shrugged like it was no big deal, but inside I was freaking out. They're trying to be friends because of me. I smiled over at Chase.

"Well, it's time I leave then. I wouldn't want to make you late for your man date."

Chase chuckled. "For that, I'm punching him when I pick him up." I looked at him with a serious face. He smiled over at me. "Aw, come on Katie, I was joking." I chuckled as I walked out of his room.

CHAPTER 28

"**B**ryan, don't make me go. I can change. I'll clean up."

"Mom, you need this. It will be good." Bryan gave his mom a hug. Two weeks after the stunt Julie pulled, Bryan set up a room for her at the rehab place in Texas and he even got one of the nurses to come pick her up. I was standing on the porch of his house watching as he said his final goodbyes to her. When Bryan pulled away from the hug, Julie put her hand on the side of his face.

"I'm so proud of you. You're just like your father." She then leaned forward and kissed his cheek before climbing into the car.

I walked up behind Bryan and slid my arm around his waist while he was watching the nurse drive his mom away. When the car was out of sight, I looked up at him. "Are you going to be okay?"

Bryan put his arm around my shoulder. "Yeah, I'll be fine." We slowly walked to the porch and sat down. After a few minutes, Bryan stood up and picked a sunflower out of one of the new flower pots. He kneeled down in front of me and said, "Katie Carpenter, will you please accompany me to the annual School's Out Carnival next weekend?"

I chuckled as I said, "Of course!" Bryan smiled as

he put his hands on both sides of my face and leaned down to kiss me. I pushed against his chest with my hand a few seconds later. "So how was your man date?" I kept my hand against his chest as I slid the other one down to find his hand before intertwining our fingers together.

He laughed as he raised his eyebrows. "He told me that you called it that." He shook his head as he looked above my head at his front yard that now seemed very quiet and super still. After a few seconds, he looked down at me. "It was fun. We went to the Yankees game, they destroyed the Pirates. Then after that, we just hung out, played some Xbox." He smiled down at me. I was about to say something when I heard a car pull up. I turned to see a yellow Hummer, Chase's yellow Hummer. I looked over at Bryan.

"Well, it must have been fun if he's here again." Bryan smiled as he lightly shrugged. He looked over at Chase and called out, "You're early!"

Chase jumped out of the car. "Hey, Katie." He walked over to me and gave me a hug before nodding toward Bryan. "You ready?"

I looked between the two guys. "What's planned for tonight, boys?"

Bryan looked down at me and chuckled. "Well, we're going to pick up girls."

When I gave Bryan a weird look, Chase interrupted, "Well, for me. See, I'm going to the carnival and I really don't wanna go alone. So if you don't mind, I need my wingman." I chuckled as I backed away.

"See you both tomorrow." I walked over to my car and before I even climbed in, Bryan and Chase were already in Chase's car driving away.

The next weekend, I was sitting on the ground and leaning against an old oak tree on one of the many hills watching the School's Out Carnival play out in front of me. It had a small petting zoo for the little kids, a hay ride around the exterior of the carnival, a lot of carnival games where you win prizes, and a ferris wheel. Food carts were set up everywhere and in the very center, there was a big white sheet that was about 35 feet by 35 feet square where they were going to show *Grease* and *Sound of Music* whenever it got dark. I looked over at the giant stuffed duck that Bryan had won for me earlier and smiled. Then out of nowhere, I heard someone's throat clear and saw Chase come out from behind the tree. He was wearing black cargo shorts with a light blue Ralph Lauren crew cut shirt and his light blue vans. I stood up and went over to hug him. "What are you doing here?"

He chuckled as he said, "Don't you mean it's nice to see you again, it's about time you got here."

"I didn't think you'd come. You said you didn't find anyone to take."

"I thought I would just come because everyone needs a third wheel." I smiled. It made my life a whole lot easier now that Bryan and Chase were friends. They hung out two times this week. On Wednesday they went to a Yankees game and then on Thursday, they went to Bryan's lake house to fish and ride Jet Ski's before heading out to see if they could find Chase a girl.

"Hey, Chase, glad you could make it, man." I looked behind me to see Bryan walking up the hill with three hot dogs in his hand and two water bottles. He was wearing navy cargo shorts with a light pink and navy striped loose tank top and navy blue vans. Chase bought those vans for Bryan as an 'I'm sorry for being a jerk' gift. After he handed me a water bottle and a hot dog, he tossed a hot dog to Chase.

Chase just smiled and said, "I guess it's better I come late than never." The three of us laughed. We all looked down the hill at the carnival that was going on. Chase stood up. "I'll be right back. I'm going to go get water." I changed positions as Bryan sat down beside me and I was now leaning against Bryan instead of leaning against the tree. I could feel him breathing. When Chase was walking back towards where we were, he was stopped by a blonde. Chase's face lit up, and a huge smile stretched across his face. I nudged Bryan, who had fallen asleep.

"Look!" Bryan sat up a little straighter and when he saw Chase, he chuckled.

"Dang, it's about time."

The way Chase was acting reminded me of something, but I couldn't quite put my finger on it. Then it hit me. "That's the way Chase acted when we first met. You see how he's smiling and the way he keeps cracking jokes? He likes her already." Chase grabbed the girl's hand as they started walking toward the carnival games. My phone beeped from inside my purse. I hadn't carried this purse since Lucas had died. I opened it up and pulled my phone out. It was a text from Chase that said, *I'll meet y'all down at the movie later. Save room on the blanket for two. :)*

I smiled and showed Bryan the text. As I was putting my phone back in my purse, something caught my eye. My old camera, it must have been in my purse all this time. I turned it on and saw a picture of Lucas and me in black and white. I paused for a second before hitting the button that said 'delete all.' Then I pressed the button that allowed me to take a picture instead of view the pictures. I saw that the setting was still on black and white, and an image of Lucas telling me that the setting black and white made life simpler ran through my mind.

But the joys in life don't come from simple times. They come from the times in life that rip your heart out. The times where you feel like you're invincible because you have that special someone with you. The joys in life are found in the complications that life offers. I switched the setting on my camera from black and white to color, because color shows life as it is. It shows every imperfection. It shows reality.

I nudged Bryan again as I said, "Let's take a picture." He nodded and kissed me on the cheek as I snapped the picture, in color, to capture the moment just as it was.

THE END

ACKNOWLEDGEMENTS

First and foremost, thank you to my Savior and best friend; Jesus Christ. Thank you for giving me the words to write and the courage to belief in myself. Also, thank you for the people I am about to mention.

Mom- Thank you for always supporting and believing in me... even when I didn't believe in myself. Thank you for never giving up on this book. I love you.

Dad- Thank you for being an open ear whenever I rambled about my book. Thank you for supporting me. I love you.

Jonah- First off, you are the best little brother on the face of the planet. You are such an inspiration. Thank you for always supporting me and making me laugh when I needed to relax. I love you and am SO proud of you.

To Brianna Huddleston, Megan Townley, Travis (Buddy) Romine, and Fredy Escobar- Thank you for letting me use your names. Thank you for always supporting me in my writing. I love each of you. Fredy- thank you for fighting for our country.

Cynthia Gustava- Thank you for being patient with me and all my grammatical errors, thank you for editing my book. Thank you for going above and beyond to help me during this process. You rock.

Jeanae Hall- Thank you for painting a picture of

what being a servant of Jesus truly means. Thank you for always being there for me, you will never know how much it has meant to me. Thank you for always cheering me on. I love you. Oh, and Jeremy Hall- sorry for stealing your wife all of those nights she was up reading this book!

Granny and Grandpa- Thank you for your never ending encouragement. You are both so special to me. I love you.

To the rest of my family- You are the reason I am who I am today. Thank you so much. I love all of you.

CPSIA information can be obtained at www.ICGtesting.com
Printed in the USA
LVOW11s0756251013

358402LV00001B/11/P